**She pressed her fing
"Shh…it's late, Neil
fight."**

Neither did he. Unfortunately they did it entirely too often. Sometimes fighting with her, matching wits with her stimulating mind, was exhilarating. Other times—when she was as stubborn as he was—fighting with her was exhausting.

And she had already admitted to being exhausted. He wasn't going to push her tonight, not when he could see how determined she was. She wasn't going to give him a win and let him put her ring back on her finger. Not tonight…

"Let's just go to bed," he suggested, and he flicked his tongue across the finger she held over his lips.

She shivered and murmured, "Neil…"

"We're alive, Elise," he reminded her. Despite someone's effort to end their lives. "Let's celebrate that tonight." And that they were having a child—whether they had decided to have it together or apart.

* * *

**The Coltons of Kansas: Truth. Justice.
And secrets they can't hide.**

* * *

**If you're on Twitter, tell us what you
think of Harlequin Romantic Suspense!
#harlequinromsuspense**

Dear Reader,

I hope your holiday season is merry and bright. For Neil Colton and Elise Willis in *Colton Christmas Conspiracy*, the season starts with a blast—a big fiery one that literally throws the divorced couple back together—as well as a bombshell of a revelation that leaves them reeling. I've had some chaotic holidays in the past myself, but nothing compares to what is thrown at the two of them— from their family and from the person or persons trying to kill them.

Despite all their turmoil, the lawyer and the mayor also find some time to decorate, bake cookies and celebrate. I am not much of a decorator, but I love to bake and celebrate. My favorite Christmas cookies are soft gingerbread with brown sugar icing. Yum. I think I will make a batch right now. A warm cookie, a cup of tea and a good read sounds like the perfect reprieve from holiday chaos for me. Hopefully you're enjoying all the books in The Coltons of Kansas series as much as I am.

Happy holidays!

Lisa Childs

COLTON CHRISTMAS CONSPIRACY

Lisa Childs

Special thanks and acknowledgment are given to Lisa Childs for her contribution to The Coltons of Kansas miniseries.

HARLEQUIN®
ROMANTIC SUSPENSE™

Recycling programs for this product may not exist in your area.

ISBN-13: 978-1-335-62677-6

Colton Christmas Conspiracy

Copyright © 2020 by Harlequin Books S.A.

This edition published by arrangement with Harlequin Books S.A.

For questions and comments about the quality of this book, please contact us at CustomerService@Harlequin.com.

Harlequin Enterprises ULC
22 Adelaide St. West, 40th Floor
Toronto, Ontario M5H 4E3, Canada
www.Harlequin.com

Printed in U.S.A.

Ever since **Lisa Childs** read her first romance novel (a Harlequin story, of course) at age eleven, all she wanted was to be a romance writer. With over seventy novels published with Harlequin, Lisa is living her dream. She is an award-winning, bestselling romance author. She loves to hear from readers, who can contact her on Facebook or through her website, lisachilds.com

Books by Lisa Childs

Harlequin Romantic Suspense

Bachelor Bodyguards

His Christmas Assignment
Bodyguard Daddy
Bodyguard's Baby Surprise
Beauty and the Bodyguard
Nanny Bodyguard
Single Mom's Bodyguard
In the Bodyguard's Arms
Soldier Bodyguard
Guarding His Witness
Evidence of Attraction
Bodyguard Boyfriend

The Coltons of Kansas

Colton Christmas Conspiracy

Colton 911

Colton 911: Baby's Bodyguard

The Coltons of Red Ridge

Colton's Cinderella Bride

Top Secret Deliveries

The Bounty Hunter's Baby Surprise

Visit the Author Profile page at Harlequin.com for more titles.

With great appreciation for all our wonderful romance readers!

Chapter 1

No. No. No.

It wasn't possible. But the little mark was there on the calendar on her desk, the mark that meant she should have started her period a couple of days ago. Sure, she was only a couple of days late, but Elise Willis was never late.

She could not be pregnant. Well, she could be…after that amazing night a month ago. But she *shouldn't* be—because that night had been a horrible mistake. A mistake that never should have happened and that could never happen again.

So why had he called?

Her fingers trembled as Elise reached for the note her assistant had left on her desk next to her calendar. Scrawled across the page from Carmen's memo pad, the note read: *Neil Colton wants you to meet him at Crest View Center.*

Crest View Center was an old warehouse that Elise and the city council had approved for renovations several months ago. But construction had been halted when dead bodies had been discovered in the walls of the basement a few months ago. It was a crime scene now, and the bodies that had been found there might not have been the only people who'd died because of the place. The health department was investigating that Colton Construction site as well as other sites Neil's father's company had renovated. And all Colton Construction operations had been suspended until the health department finished their investigation.

Was that why Neil wanted her to meet him there? Did he think that she, as the mayor of Braxville, Kansas, could somehow help his family?

A chuckle slipped out at the irony of a mayor helping Fitz Colton, Neil's hardheaded father. He'd hated her predecessor, former employer and mentor, and he probably did not think too highly of her, either. But that might have had less to do with her job than her former marriage…to his son.

Neil…

Her pulse quickened at the thought of seeing her exhusband again. Dare she meet with him?

Hell, all she had to do to see Neil was close her eyes. Every time she did, he appeared with his bright blue eyes, dark brown hair and that faint scruff of reddish-brown beard clinging to his chiseled, stubborn jaw. He was too damn good-looking.

Always had been, from the first moment she'd noticed him across a law school lecture hall. When he'd caught her staring at him, she had quickly turned away from him. But it had been too late—despite her determination to stay focused on her education and on establishing her career.

"Mayor Willis," her assistant called, drawing Elise's attention to the open doorway to her office where Carmen stood, her purse dangling from her shoulder. She was a little older than Elise, with a few silver strands winding through the dark curls that brushed her shoulders. Her eyes were dark, too, and warm like her personality. "Is it all right if I leave now?"

Elise nodded. "Of course. You stayed later than you needed to."

"The phones don't stop ringing," Carmen said with a weary-sounding sigh.

"I know…"

Braxville was in crisis right now and not just because of the dead bodies that had been uncovered at Crest View Center. Those old murders were less of a concern than more people getting sick. Too many residents, most of them current or former Colton Construction workers, had cancer. A couple had even died.

Years ago, Colton Construction had renovated another old warehouse into what was now Ruby Row shopping center. If the mall truly was contaminated, like the state health department inspector—who was also Elise's ex-sister-in-law—was concerned that it was, then she would have no choice but to shut it down during the busiest shopping season of the year, Christmas.

But the results of Bridgette's tests weren't back yet. Every time the phone rang Elise worried that it was her calling to confirm contamination.

"Are you all right?" Carmen asked with concern.

Elise nodded. Maybe all the stress was the reason why she'd missed her period. Maybe it had nothing to do with what had happened last month…between her and her ex-husband. She held up the message her assistant had taken. "Did Neil say anything else when he called?"

"He didn't call," Carmen said. "Someone from his office did."

Someone from his office…

Who?

Elise knew most of them since that office had once been hers, too. She preferred this one, though, with its coffered ceiling and dark-paneled walls, mostly because she had it all to herself. But it was late, and she needed to leave. Should she go meet Neil, though?

"So no reason for the meeting was given?" Elise asked.

Carmen shook her head. "And I didn't feel right asking since he's your…" Color flushed her face as her words trailed off.

"Ex-husband," Elise finished for her. That had been his decision, not hers. He was the one who'd given up on them—on her. So if she didn't show up to this meeting he'd proposed, he would probably give up again.

But because they'd once been partners, in more than marriage, they'd vowed to try to remain friends. She glanced into the purse she'd dropped next to her chair. The leather bag gaped open, revealing the box she'd bought at the pharmacy that morning—the pregnancy test.

If only they'd remained *just* friends…

She needed to take that test. She needed to know.

"Are you sure you're all right?" Carmen asked again.

Elise forced a smile and nodded. "Yes, I'm fine. Please, go home to your family."

In addition to her three kids and husband, Carmen's in-laws also lived with her, which might have been why she didn't really seem to mind working late. At least she had help at home, though.

Unlike Elise's mother, who'd raised her alone. Was that how Elise would raise her child, if she was pregnant? She grabbed up her purse from beside her desk and slid the strap over her shoulder. She needed to talk to Neil and not just to find out why the hell he wanted her to meet him at a crime scene. Given the way they tended to communicate, though, the place might wind up being a crime scene once again.

"So Crest View Center, the warehouse, isn't a crime scene anymore?" Neil asked his older sister for confirmation.

"No, Yvette and the rest of the techs thoroughly processed the site for evidence months ago," Jordana said, her voice emanating from the speaker of his cell phone.

The glow from it illuminated the dark interior of his SUV. He'd shut off the lights some time ago while he waited in the parking lot for Elise to arrive.

"So I'll be able to get inside?" he asked.

"Yeah, if you have a key to it," Jordana said. "Did

Dad give you one? Why the hell would you want to go there anyway? You know Bridgette took samples from it to test for contamination?"

"Yeah, I know," he said. "She doesn't have the results back, though." Unless she'd contacted Elise before anyone else in the family.

But if the place was contaminated, why would Elise have wanted to meet him there?

"So why are you going there?" Jordana asked. Then she gasped aloud, and it echoed inside his vehicle. "You're not representing Markus Dexter, are you?"

"Has he been arrested?" Neil asked, hoping like hell that he had been.

"No," she said. "But has he been in contact with you? Did he try to hire you?"

"I damn well think he would know better than to try to hire me after he shot my brother," Neil said. Not to mention how he'd betrayed his business partner, Neil's father, as well.

"If he hasn't hired you, why are you so interested in the crime scene?" Jordana asked with suspicion, like he was a suspect the Braxville detective was interviewing.

A criminal lawyer, he was often present at those interviews. Being the interviewee had him smiling with amusement. "I'm not interested in it." In fact, he was kind of loath to find out anything else about his father's business and his business partner. "I'm meeting someone here." And before she could ask again, he assured her, "It's not Dexter."

"Then who?" she asked.

"The mayor," he replied.

Her sigh rattled the cell now. "Of course."

"What does that mean?" he asked.

She sighed again. "Just that the two of you have some strange divorce."

He couldn't deny that they did, not after what had happened between them last month. "We're friends."

"With friends like that, who needs enemies?"

"Just because we got divorced doesn't make Elise my enemy," he assured his overprotective sister. Despite only being a year older than he and the other triplets, Jordana acted like she had to take care of all of them. Maybe because of her military background…

"Dad might not agree with you," Jordana warned him.

His father always struggled with mayors, but it didn't help that Elise was determined to carry on her predecessor's legacy of limiting urban sprawl. But that wasn't the only thing adversely affecting his father's construction business right now. There were also the open investigations by the police department and the health department.

That was why he hadn't taken on any new clients lately; he was going to wait to see what happened with his family. And with Elise.

He sighed. "I'm sure you're busy, Jordana, so I'll let you go now."

She was stammering something in protest when he clicked off the cell. But he didn't want to hear whatever his older sister had to say about his ex-wife any more than he ever wanted to hear what his father had to say about Elise and her politics. His family didn't understand Elise like he did.

He chuckled at his own joke. Hell, he didn't understand her, either. Never had. Probably never would.

He stared through his windshield at the dark building. Why the hell did Elise want to meet him here? So there would not be a repeat of what had happened the last time they'd met?

That was a damn shame.

His body tensed just remembering what had happened that night—how a friendly hug good-night had turned into a hot embrace.

A brush of his mouth across her soft lips…

He groaned—like he had that night—as desire overwhelmed him. Hell, he didn't care where she wanted to meet—just that she wanted to meet again. He needed to see her…see her beautiful face, her green eyes sparkling with amusement and intelligence as she challenged him, as she always challenged him.

That was probably why she'd left the message for him to meet her here—to challenge him about something to do with his family. He was aware that one of his sisters—his fellow triplet Bridgette—had talked to her about the health department's concerns regarding all Colton Construction projects, including the mall. But he and Elise had agreed, during their last meeting, to not talk about his family or city business…which was probably how they'd wound up making love instead. They'd had nothing left to argue about.

Yet they weren't ever able to completely agree on anything.

His mouth slid into a grin, though, as he remembered the lobbying for position, her pushing him onto his back so she could straddle him…her long golden hair falling in a curtain around them both as she leaned down, brushing her breasts over his chest as she pressed her mouth to his.

He groaned again, and his body throbbed with need—need for her. He wanted her so damn badly. Always had.

Probably always would. Damn it.

But Elise didn't want him. At least not for more than that one, passionate night last month.

So why had she called him here tonight? Was it possible that she'd finally changed her mind about them? That she wanted what he wanted now.

No. Elise did not change her mind once she'd made it up. She had undoubtedly called this meeting about his family.

If she wanted to talk about the possible health hazards of the Colton Construction projects, why not call Bridgette? Or his father?

He groaned again, but it had nothing to do with desire now, just dread. Elise and his father had never gotten along. It was clear that she suspected Fitz Colton was more involved with what had happened in this building, with what his business partner had done, than he was willing to admit.

And Neil was afraid she might be right. That was why they'd banned the topic of the Coltons during their last monthly dinner. But apparently she thought that ban had expired.

Lights illuminated the warehouse as another car pulled into the lot. He recognized the two-door compact as Elise's little vehicle, and he wished again that she would drive something bigger, safer.

But if he suggested as much, again, she would accuse him of being controlling or overprotective. If only they could agree not to argue every time they'd met, like they'd agreed last month.

If only they could do *that* every time they got together…

He had no such expectations for this meeting, though—not when she'd called it here. She must have been in a hurry to get it started, because she pushed open the driver's door and stepped into the parking lot. Because of the tinted windows, she must not have noticed him sitting inside his SUV, since she headed straight toward the building.

He sucked in a breath over her walk. At five-six, she wasn't tall, but her legs were long enough that she moved quickly and easily, her hips rolling beneath her tightly cinched trench coat. He wanted to imagine that she wore nothing beneath the coat, that that was the reason for asking him to meet her. But why here?

Of all places?

He had only one way of finding out—to actually ask her. So he pushed open the door to his SUV and stepped out. A sudden chill rushed over him. Maybe it was the cold night air. Maybe it was something else…

He glanced around the lot. Was somebody out there? Because he had the sudden, unsettling sensation that someone was watching him.

* * *

He watched them from the shadows at the far corner of the parking lot. He watched first the woman as she walked into the building, into the trap he'd set for them. Then, finally, the man got out of his vehicle. But Neil Colton hesitated a long moment.

And his head turned from side to side as he looked around the lot, as if he somehow sensed his presence. He held his breath, not daring to move even his lungs in case he was discovered.

His plan could not fall apart now, not when he was just getting started with it. He'd waited too long and had planned too well. And he'd chosen to start with the couple because they would be the easiest to eliminate.

They were lawyers. Book-smart. Not street-smart. But the man was more cautious than he'd thought he would be. But then he was a Colton.

The Colton family had reason to be cautious since bodies had already been discovered in this building.

Finally the man stopped looking around and headed toward the warehouse, too.

He wrapped his hand around the detonator he held. How long should he wait before he pressed the button? How long before he ended their miserable lives?

Chapter 2

A chill chased down Elise's spine as she walked farther inside the abandoned warehouse. The door was unlocked, and she'd noticed Neil's SUV parked in the lot. She'd purposely parked a distance away from it because she remembered what had happened the last time she'd parked next to him. What had happened when they'd left the restaurant and walked back to their vehicles.

The hug that had turned into more...

The kiss.

The passion between them had drawn her to him, her body demanding the pleasure and the release she knew he could give her. And damn, after dealing with everything that had happened in Braxville over the past few months, she had desperately needed that release, that mindless pleasure.

But she should have known that there were always consequences for her actions. What would be the consequence for coming here?

Would it end as that night last month had ended? In his bed? Her pulse quickened at the thought, but it wasn't racing just with excitement but also with fear. She couldn't get used to going home with him—to the home they'd designed and had his father's company build for them after they'd settled in Braxville.

She was not going to go home with him. That wouldn't be a consequence of this meeting. But getting hurt might be.

She stumbled over something in the dark. The only light in the warehouse came from her phone. Where was Neil?

"Hello?" she called out, her voice echoing off the brick walls and concrete floor. "Hello?"

Was it safe to even be here?

Neil's triplet, Bridgette, had insisted that construction not start again on the warehouse until her investigation was complete. What kind of contaminants might be in this place?

Elise ran a hand protectively over her stomach. Could coming here cause problems with her potential pregnancy? Was it safe healthwise?

She needed to get the hell out of here, but she hadn't realized how far she'd walked into the warehouse until she heard the far-off creak of a door opening. If that sound had come from the outside door, she'd walked quite a distance into the building without even realizing it. But then she'd been lost in thought, in memories…

She pushed those from her mind now as she turned toward the noise she heard and the faint light moving toward her. A big shadow loomed behind it, and her pulse leaped again with fear and excitement.

"Neil?"

It had to be Neil; he was the one who'd asked her to meet him here. Then her excitement waned until just the fear gripped her.

"Neil? Is that you?"

"Elise?" he called back to her. "Damn, it's dark in here." He must have been using his cell phone as light, too, because only a small beam moved toward her with that shadow behind it. "Why did you want to meet here?"

"Me?" She tensed with indignation and uneasiness. "You were the one who wanted to meet here."

Even during their divorce, she and Neil had never played any games with each other. They'd civilly handled separating their personal and professional lives. So why would he be playing games with her now? Or wasn't he the one who was playing?

That strange sensation that Neil had had earlier overwhelmed him now. He'd suspected then that something wasn't right about this meeting, at this location. It hadn't made sense then and made less now.

"What?" he asked. "I didn't ask you to meet me here. You asked me."

She shook her head, whipping her long hair around her shoulders. "I did not. You said to meet here."

"When?" he asked. "I didn't call you. You were the one who called—"

"I did not!" she interjected. "You had someone from the office call and leave a message—"

"Who?" he asked. "Who called? You know everybody." She had helped him hire everyone, and all the staff—albeit small—had stayed with him. She was the only one who'd left the practice.

"I didn't answer the phone. Carmen did."

"So this person didn't call your cell? They called the main switchboard for City Hall?"

"You know who this person is," she persisted. "You had them make the call for you."

He shook his head now. "No. I didn't. I also received a message my assistant took…from someone from the mayor's office." He cursed. "I should have known."

"What?" she asked, her eyes wide in the dim light.

"That you would have called me directly if you wanted to see me." But he'd thought that she might have been embarrassed, after what had happened the last time they saw each other.

But he should have known better. Elise didn't get embarrassed. She was strong, independent and, most of all, direct.

She cursed now. "And you would have done the same if you'd really wanted to see me. I should have known."

But she must have initially drawn the same wrong conclusion he had—that their night together last month had made him uncomfortable. He wasn't uncomfortable, though, except for the frustration gripping his body. He needed another release like she'd given him that night—one so intense it had shaken him to his core.

"So what's the deal?" she asked. "Why would someone leave those messages for us?"

He shrugged. "Maybe they're playing matchmaker? Trying to get us back together."

She chuckled, emitting that throaty sound that had always driven him wild with desire. "Nobody we know actually wants us back together," she said.

"Your mother," he said, a smile curving his lips as he thought of her.

"Yes, but she's too busy with her college classes to play matchmaker." Her voice was soft with pride and happiness that her mother was finally getting the education she'd been denied when she'd been forced to raise her daughter alone. "And she's too far away, back in Michigan, to be meddling in our lives."

Her mother was not a meddler. She also knew her daughter too well to try.

Elise continued, "And your family certainly isn't going to play matchmaker for us."

"My mother loves you," he insisted. "And my siblings—"

She chuckled again. "Your mother, yes, but not your siblings. I don't know if they liked me before the divorce, but now they certainly don't."

He sighed. "I don't even know if they like me half the time, so don't worry about it."

"I don't," she said, but her brow furrowed, and she glanced around the warehouse. "I am worried that someone tricked us into showing up here, though."

"Me, too." He glanced around, but he couldn't see anyone else in the place. And he didn't feel like he had outside, where he'd sensed someone had been watching him.

"Let's get out of here," Elise said with a sudden shudder.

When she headed toward the door they'd entered, Neil caught her arm and pulled her back. "Not that way."

"But the door is that way," she said.

"Was it unlocked?" he asked. It had looked like she'd walked right in.

She nodded.

"I don't like this…"

"Me, neither," she agreed. "So let's get the hell out of here."

"There's got to be another way out of here," he said. "One that doesn't open onto the parking lot."

"What are you worried about?"

"Dexter is still on the loose," Neil said. "This feels like a setup, and I thought I felt someone outside, watching the warehouse."

She sucked in a shaky-sounding breath. "Okay…"

He raised his phone and waved it around the space until the faint light reflected off a sign on the other side of the building: EXIT.

"This way," he said, and he tugged her through the warehouse toward the sign. At the door, he pushed against the steel, but it didn't budge. And another curse slipped through his lips.

"Push it down," she said.

But before he could figure out what she meant, she shoved him aside and slammed her hands against the handle, which was a bar stretching across the steel. The bar popped and the door opened.

A cold breeze blowing across the field behind the warehouse wafted inside the brick building, stirring dust and another strange smell. It could have been anything—since some of the construction materials might have been substandard, or so his sister Bridgette suspected. But this building had been abandoned before it could be renovated like the mall and some other structures in town.

The smell that tickled his nose didn't come from building materials, though. It reminded him of the times his father had convinced Neil to go hunting with him—of gunpowder!

A sudden urgency came over Neil, and he grabbed Elise's arm again, pulling her along with him as he ran through the door and away from the building.

"What the hell…" Elise murmured in protest, gasping for breath as they waded into thick, dead weeds in the small field behind the building. "You know I don't exer—"

She stopped talking as the ground shook and shuddered beneath them. Then the building exploded, bits of glass and debris propelling toward them. The force of the blast knocked them to the ground. Then flames reached out, too, like tendrils trying to pull them back—into the fire.

But then everything started going dark for Neil as he struggled for consciousness. He had to make sure that Elise was all right—had to make sure that whoever had been watching them didn't realize they'd gone out the back way. That they'd escaped the blast.

But had they?

His ears buzzed from the explosion as dizziness overwhelmed him. He was only able to murmur, "Elise…" And hope that she was all right, before consciousness slipped away from him.

"Dexter might be back!" Reese Carpenter said, his deep voice rattling Jordana's phone.

She smiled apologetically at her date—and the love of her life, Clint Broderick—and mouthed the words, "I'm sorry."

She really needed to stop answering her cell, though. Clint, determined to stop obsessing over business, always shut his off now when they were together. She would have done the same…if not for her job. A detective needed to be available, especially when there was a suspected killer on the loose.

"Dexter? Where was he seen?" she asked.

Clint tensed and sat up straighter in the chair across the candlelit table from her. The flame of the candle illuminated a flicker of concern in his blue eyes. He worried about her, but he also trusted that she could take care of herself.

Damn. She was lucky she'd found him—that they'd found each other. If only they had more time together.

His business was in Chicago, but he came back to Braxville every weekend to stay with her. If only she wasn't so damn busy.

"Nobody reported actually seeing him but dispatch

just got a call about an explosion at the warehouse where the bodies were found. He must be trying to destroy evidence." Reese chuckled. "Idiot. It's too late for that. Yvette wouldn't have missed anything."

"Neil!" Jordana exclaimed as she jumped up from the table. Other diners whirled around to stare at her in alarm. She was aware she'd attracted some attention since she walked in but wasn't sure if it was because they knew she was a detective or because they knew she was a Colton.

Clint jumped up, as well, and tossed some bills next to his untouched plate of food. She would have told him to stay, to finish eating, if she wasn't so damn worried that something had happened to her brother.

"What about Neil?" Reese asked.

Her heart pounded fast and hard with fear. "He was meeting the mayor at the warehouse."

"Why?"

"I don't know," she said. She headed toward the door with Clint sticking close beside her. "But send an ambulance out to Crest View, too."

"Jordana…" Reese began.

More dread gripped her. The explosion must have been big, so big that her partner doubted anyone could have survived it. But they had to have.

She couldn't have lost her brother. And despite their divorce, Elise was still family, too. They had to be okay. They had to be…

Chapter 3

Was he in shock? Or was he seriously wounded?

Elise closed her eyes as she remembered those first moments after the blast when she'd rolled to her side to see if Neil was all right.

His eyes had been closed, his body shockingly still for a man who was usually always in motion. Neil paced his office. He paced a courtroom. He even moved in his sleep. But now...

He was so still.

So lifeless.

She forced her eyes open to assess him, to see if his life was truly gone.

"Neil!" she shouted at him over the roar of the flames, over the ringing in her ears and the pounding of her heart.

And he blinked open his eyes to stare at her with first confusion, then concern. "Are you all right?" he asked, his first question about her. But he was that way, always fiercely protective and defensive of everyone else.

She flopped onto her back in the scratchy weeds and considered...

She could move. She hadn't lost consciousness. But what about the baby? Was the baby all right?

If there even was a baby.

There was.

She knew it—even without being able to feel anything. She knew she was pregnant, that she was carrying the child Neil had always wanted. If she hadn't lost it from the explosion propelling them to the ground.

"What the hell happened?" she mused aloud.

"We were set up," Neil said, his voice gruff.

Wondering at his paranoia, she turned back to him. Surely the explosion had just been an accident. "Are *you* all right?" she asked. The glow from the burning building illuminated his handsome face. His hair was mussed and matted with bits of debris and weeds. But she couldn't see any obvious injuries.

He levered himself up to his knees and nodded. "I'm fine. But we need to get the hell out of here."

"How?" she asked.

Had their vehicles survived the blast? They'd been parked fairly close to the building. If he hadn't dragged her along with him to the exit and out to this field...

But she could feel more than dirt beneath her. The weeds had grown up through the crumbling asphalt of an old parking lot. Using the asphalt as leverage, she pushed her hands against it and sat up. Then she stared at the building. Flames rose through gaping holes in the roof. At the realization that they could have been inside, buried under debris, burned, she shuddered.

"You saved my life," she murmured in awe. "How did you know this was going to happen?"

He stared at the devastation, too. "I didn't know this was going to happen," he said. "But those messages luring us here were obviously a setup for something."

"Certainly not for matchmaking," she murmured with another tremor of fear.

"And I felt somebody outside watching us," he added. "Probably waiting for this…" He gestured toward the building with a hand that shook.

"Do you think it was Markus Dexter?" she asked. His dad's business partner was the prime suspect in the murders of the people whose bodies had been discovered in that very warehouse. So it must have been him.

Neil just continued to stare at the fire.

The most important thing she wanted to know, though, was "Why us?"

He shook his head. "I don't know. I just know we need to get out of here in case he's still around."

Sirens wailed and lights flashed on the road behind the field, which was really an abandoned parking lot, as fire trucks and police cruisers approached.

"If Dexter was still here, he'll leave now," she told Neil.

But she needed assurances herself. She slid her hand over her stomach.

And Neil's hand followed hers, covering it. "Are you hurt? Did something hit you?"

Fear. She was so damn scared. She hadn't even been sure that she wanted a baby…until now. She wanted *this* baby.

Neil didn't wait for her reply. He closed his arms around her and lifted her up as he staggered to his feet. She didn't know if it was because she wasn't all that light or if he had been hurt.

"I can walk," she told him.

"You don't like exercise," he reminded her, his lips curving into a slight grin.

God, she…

Was so relieved that he was all right. Wasn't he?

He stumbled again, but maybe he'd just gotten caught up in the dead weeds pulling at his legs and at their clothes, as he walked through the abandoned rear parking lot and headed toward the front of the building. Before he rounded the corner, people emerged from the shadows into the glow of the fire.

Paramedics rushed toward them. "Are you all right?" a male EMT echoed the question Neil had asked of Elise.

"I—I don't know," she stammered, fear gripping her even tighter than Neil held her in his arms.

The man shone a small light in her eyes. "Did you hit your head? Lose consciousness?"

She squinted against the light, tears springing to her eyes. "No. But he might have," she said, gesturing toward Neil.

The light turned toward his face.

"I'm fine," Neil insisted.

"You must not have been inside the building, then," the female EMT remarked as she stared at the burning structure.

Neil shook his head, "No."

"So neither of you need treatment?" the male EMT asked.

"I—I might…" Elise continued to stammer over the words that she needed to say, just in case…she was carrying Neil's child.

But she hadn't wanted to tell him until she knew for certain and had had a chance to process for herself. And when she told him, she hadn't wanted it to be like this. The explosion had taken that choice away from her, though, and had potentially put her unborn child at risk. She had to know for sure that the baby was all right.

She drew in a deep breath and finished, "I might be pregnant."

Neil tensed and sucked in a breath, as well. Then, still clutching her closely in his arms, he strode toward the front of the burning building, where the ambulance was parked among police vehicles—all with lights flashing. He lifted her through the open back doors of the ambulance and laid her on the gurney sitting inside it.

Would he drop her and leave? Was he angry? She stared at his face, but he was stoic. Then he settled onto a bench seat on one side of the ambulance, as if to make it clear that he wasn't going anywhere.

The male paramedic jumped into the back of the ambulance while the female one climbed into the driver's seat. She turned back and asked, "Nobody else was hurt in the explosion?"

Maybe she thought someone else might need help more than Elise did. She slid her hand over her stomach again, already protective of the child she might be carrying. "There was nobody else inside the building," she said. "Nobody that we saw as we ran out of it anyway."

There could have been someone else, though.

"If someone was inside the building, they probably didn't survive," the male paramedic remarked as he slid an oxygen sensor onto the tip of one of her fingers before wrapping a blood pressure cuff around her arm. "Let's head to the hospital."

Yes. Now finally Elise would have the confirmation she needed—that she was pregnant, and if she was, that the baby was all right.

He or she had to be all right.

Was Neil? He was so quiet. Maybe he had been hurt during the explosion. She'd thought he'd lost consciousness for a moment, like the paramedic had suspected. So had he hit his head on the asphalt?

Fumbling with the oxygen sensor on her finger, she clasped the paramedic's arm and murmured, "Please make sure he gets checked out, too. We were knocked down from the blast."

The paramedic glanced at Neil and nodded. "He could also be in shock."

But maybe Neil wasn't quiet because he was hurt or in shock. Maybe it was because of what she'd just had to admit to the paramedic. That she could be carrying his child…

* * *

Neil was in shock. So much so that he didn't move when the doors opened onto the ambulance bay at the ER. The paramedics whisked Elise out on the stretcher and disappeared with her down a hallway before he realized they were taking her away from him.

Dazed, he lurched to his feet and jumped down from the ambulance. Weakness had overtaken his leg muscles since he'd been sitting for a while, causing him to dodder as he walked toward the entrance to the ER.

"Sir," a nurse exclaimed, rushing to him. "Are you all right?"

He shook his head.

No.

Not now…

"Let me get a wheelchair for you," she said. "Or a stretcher."

He shook his head again. "No, I have to find my…" Wife. The word nearly slipped off his tongue. But she wasn't his wife anymore. What was she?

Pregnant? She might be pregnant.

Was that possible? She was always so vigilant about taking her birth control—so much so that she'd assured him last month that it was fine that he didn't have a condom. She wasn't seeing anyone else anyway.

So if she was pregnant…

The baby was his. His and Elise's.

That was once all he'd wanted, so he should have been overjoyed. But instead, he was just shocked. And scared…

What if something had happened to the baby? What

if she actually wasn't pregnant? What if she was but didn't want the baby any more than she had when they'd divorced three years ago?

She hadn't been pregnant then. She'd refused to get pregnant…until she was ready. Neil had suspected that she would never be ready, and he hadn't wanted to fight about it anymore, or worse yet, turn into the painfully civil, cohabiting strangers his parents were. So he had filed for divorce.

Elise hadn't fought him on that like she usually fought him on everything. Apparently, the divorce was one of the few things on which they'd agreed.

"Sir," the nurse spoke to him again with an urgency in her voice, as if she'd called out to him a few times. She had a wheelchair now and tried to ease him into it.

But he shook his head again. "I don't need treatment."

He needed answers.

He needed to make sure that Elise and his…baby… were all right. "The paramedics just brought back a woman. I have to find where they've taken her, see how she's doing."

"I'll check on her for you while you're being seen," the nurse offered. "You were at the explosion?"

He nodded. "With her. We were already out of the building when it exploded, though." But had they gotten far enough from it before the big blast? Had anything hit Elise? How hard had she been knocked to the ground? He'd hit it so hard that the air had momentarily left his lungs, and he hadn't been able to draw in another breath. That was probably why consciousness had slipped away from him for a minute, because he hadn't been able to breathe.

"You should still be checked out," the nurse insisted, and she shoved a little harder on his shoulder, trying to push him into the wheelchair.

The weakness had left his legs now, and he had no problem walking. But he didn't get far before another woman joined the nurse.

She wore scrubs, as well, with a name tag on the pocket that he didn't need to read. He knew her better than any other woman in the world.

Her blue eyes glistening with tears of concern, she pulled him into a tight embrace. "Neil!" his mother exclaimed, and her slender frame trembled. "Are you all right?"

"Yes," he insisted as he pulled away from her. "I'm fine."

"Really?" She scrutinized his face, furrows forming in her forehead. She wore her dark auburn hair up in some type of messy bun. Her fingers trembled as she ran them lightly over his face, knocking dirt and briars from his short beard. "What happened?"

"We got knocked down—by the explosion," he admitted.

Then she knocked him down, gently shoving him into the wheelchair the other nurse had failed to get him to use. His mother didn't give him a choice. "You are getting checked out," she insisted.

"I'm—"

"A lawyer," she interjected. "Not a medical professional. We're going to let someone else evaluate your health."

She propelled him down the hall and through double doors that opened automatically onto a big room. A nurses' station sat to the left, while the rest of the area was cordoned off with walls that didn't reach entirely to the tall ceiling. Each of those walled-off cubes had a curtain that was either pulled open or shut.

Elise had to be in here, too. The paramedics must have rolled her back into one of the walled-off spaces. He glanced around, but he couldn't see behind the closed curtains.

"Where's Elise?" he asked his mother. "I need to find her."

"Elise was with you?" Lilly asked with concern. "Is she all right?"

"That's what I need to know," he said. "But where is she? Please, Mom, find out what's going on with her."

His mother's voice, which had been all warm concern, changed to chilly professionalism. "I can't tell you her medical condition."

He jumped up from the wheelchair and whirled toward her. "Why the hell can't you?"

"Privacy laws—"

"She's my wife."

"She *was* your wife," his mother corrected him. "She isn't anymore. She has every right to her privacy."

"But…"

"But what?" his mother prodded.

"She might be carrying my child," he admitted.

His mother's mouth dropped open as she drew in a sharp breath. Then a smile curved her lips. "That's…"

"Surprising," he finished for her.

She shook her head. "No, not really, not with how close you two have remained even since the divorce."

"So find out where she is and how she is," he persisted. "I need to know that there's nothing wrong with her or the baby." *And that there is a baby…*

Elise had told the paramedic that she wasn't certain she was pregnant. But she was never late, either. He knew that from when they'd lived together.

His mother's hands closed around his shoulders as she moved him toward one of those partitioned-off areas with an open curtain. She pushed him onto the stretcher and said, "Sit down and get checked out."

The other nurse must have summoned a doctor, because one joined them now, firing questions at him that he ignored. Fortunately, they hadn't closed his curtain, so he could peer around the open area. Maybe he had to pull open every other curtain to find Elise. She was all he could focus on right now.

As if his mother had read his mind, she said, "You're going to stay here and get examined, and when Elise has been released, she can update you on her condition… if she chooses to."

"But if something's happened, she might need me," he said, but the words sounded hollow even as he uttered them. Elise had never needed him; in fact, she'd done much better without him in her life.

She'd gone from being his partner in a fledgling law firm to running the whole damn town. Had she been the target of the bomb? It had to have been a bomb that had caused the explosion. Someone must have rigged up one in the abandoned warehouse and lured them there.

"She could still be in danger," he said, panic pressing on his madly pounding heart as the thought finally occurred to him. Maybe he had struck his head when the blast pushed him to the ground. Maybe that was why he hadn't considered that the bomber could have followed the ambulance away from the burning warehouse.

"We have good security," his mother said with pride in the hospital at which she spent so much time. He could understand that she would prefer being here to spending time at home with his father. There had always been so much tension in their house, but it had to be even worse now, because of the ongoing investigation.

"The security might be good, but I don't trust anyone," Neil said. Not with the life of Elise and their unborn child. "I can't…"

"Being a criminal lawyer has made you cynical," she admonished him.

"Being a criminal lawyer has made me a realist," he corrected her. He knew there were really bad people in the world. She had to know that, too, as a nurse.

But his mother always insisted on finding the good in everyone. Maybe that was why she'd stayed with his father so long, even though they clearly weren't happy.

"The police are also on their way to question you about what happened," his mother said. "You do trust your sister, right?"

He groaned. "Jordana called you," he said. That was why their mother had rushed to the ER area, when usually she was involved only in training and administration now.

"She knew you were going to the warehouse," Mom said. "And when she learned about the explosion, she got worried."

"She's not the only one," he bitterly remarked. He was worried, too, so damn worried about Elise.

The flashing lights and blaring sirens on the ambulance had drawn him to follow as it sped away from the burning warehouse. Somebody was hurt.

Not dead...

They were supposed to be dead. They couldn't have survived the explosion. Unless...

Had they been inside?

He'd watched them enter the building—falling into the trap he'd set for them—but had they exited some other way? Had they escaped before he'd detonated the bomb? If they had, they would not be so damn freakishly lucky the next time.

And there would be a next time.

He wasn't going to stop until they were dead.

Chapter 4

"You're sure?" Elise asked, anxiety fluttering through her stomach. Or was that fluttering she felt due to some other reason? No. It was too soon for her to feel the baby move. It might have been the ultrasound wand they'd had to insert inside her, though. The young female resident had informed Elise that at approximately four weeks, she wasn't far enough along for them to see anything with a traditional ultrasound.

"Your blood work confirms you're pregnant," the resident said as she read the results the nurse had brought to her.

"But is the baby all right?" Elise needed to know.

"You're not bleeding, and you've said you have no pain?"

She shook her head. "No. No pain," she confirmed. Just fear...

The doctor moved that wand inside her and something appeared on the machine's monitor. Elise stared at it, but she couldn't see anything. Tears stung her eyes. She hadn't realized how much she'd wanted to be pregnant. "There's nothing there. Are you sure...?"

The doctor pointed at the screen. "This...this is the gestational sac."

"What is that?"

"It's where the fetus is developing," she said. "It's intact. Your pregnancy is definitely still viable."

"The explosion didn't hurt...him or her?"

"It's way too soon to tell the gender," the doctor said as she pulled out the wand. The image remained on the screen, though.

"I'm not worried about the gender," Elise said. She didn't really care. "I just want to make sure the baby's all right."

"You're in the early stages of development, so you don't need to worry about injuries to the fetus. You have no injuries, so I see no risk of a miscarriage from what happened tonight."

Elise expelled a shaky sigh of relief. "Thank you."

"I had nothing to do with it," the doctor replied. "I'm just the messenger."

It was Neil who had saved her life, his and their baby's. She owed him her gratitude. She owed him the truth. "How is the man who came into the ER with me?" she asked.

But he hadn't actually come in with her. When the paramedics had whisked her out of the ambulance, Neil must have remained inside it. He hadn't followed her. Was he really all right? He'd been knocked down even harder than she had. And when she'd first called to him, he hadn't immediately responded. Had he lost consciousness briefly? Did he have a concussion?

"Man?" the doctor asked.

"She's talking about my son," she heard a voice say as the curtain slid aside.

Elise closed her eyes for a moment, but when she opened them, Lilly Colton was there in the small ER space with them. Not that Elise disliked the woman...

Lilly was actually Elise's favorite Colton. But she couldn't deal with her now, not when she was reeling from everything else. And Neil deserved to know before his mother did, that he was going to be a father.

Lilly's blue eyes, so like her son's, were focused on the monitor and that strange bubble that had remained on the screen even after the doctor removed the wand. Unlike Elise, who had no idea what she was looking at, Lilly, as a nurse, must have recognized the image. A soft sigh slipped out of the older woman's lips.

The young doctor lowered her voice and stepped closer to Lilly. "Should you be in here, since you know her?"

"No," Lilly admitted. "I stopped Neil from barging in and then I..."

"It's okay," Elise said, even though she wasn't entirely sure about that herself.

The doctor looked at Elise for a moment, as if assessing the situation. "If you're sure..."

"I am," Elise said.

And Lilly released another little sigh. "I'll help her get dressed," she told the doctor, "while you write up your release orders."

The doctor hesitated yet.

"She is being released?" Lilly asked with concern.

"Of course," Elise answered for her. "You told me that I'm fine."

The doctor nodded and finally stepped out of the small area, pulling the curtain closed behind her as if she suspected she and her former mother-in-law needed privacy.

"She's right," Lilly said as she stepped closer to the gurney. "I probably shouldn't be in here, but she's a resident who comes from a big city, so she doesn't realize that most of the staff here winds up having to treat people we know. Even though we do, we abide by the privacy laws, and we don't share what we learn." Lilly covered Elise's hand with hers and gently squeezed. "This is your business. No one else's."

"I wish…" Elise murmured ruefully, but she hadn't conceived this baby via artificial insemination.

"Even the mayor is entitled to privacy," Lilly assured her.

Elise groaned. She hadn't considered yet that being an unwed mother could impact her career, at least in a town as conservative as Braxville. Fortunately she had a few years to go on her term before needing to worry about a reelection campaign. "I wasn't worried about voters, at least not all of them. Just one…"

But had Neil voted for her?

If he had, he'd probably been the only Colton, with

the probable exception of her ex-mother-in-law. Lilly had always been very sweet and affectionate and welcoming to her. The other Coltons had been, too, until the divorce and until she'd gone to work for her predecessor.

"If you're talking about Neil..."

"I know," Elise said. "You're his mother, and your loyalty will always be to him."

"My loyalty is to all my family," Lilly said. "And you will always be family."

"So is this baby," Elise confessed as she moved her hand, still clasped in Lilly's, to her stomach. "This is Neil's baby."

Lilly smiled, but there was no surprise on her face. She'd already known. Neil must have sent her back to check on Elise or maybe just on his unborn child. A baby was all he'd really wanted from her, not the complete partnership he'd promised, or he would have given her the time she'd wanted before starting a family.

"I already informed him about the privacy laws that preclude him from learning your medical condition. I won't tell him anything," Lilly promised.

"I will," Elise assured her.

"Take your time," Lilly advised. "Make your decisions based on your needs, nobody else's. You have to do what's going to make you happy. Life's too short to live with regrets."

Surprise widened Elise's eyes. "I didn't expect you to say that to me."

"Because I'm Neil's mother?"

Elise nodded.

Lilly released her hand and stepped back from

the gurney, and she murmured wistfully, "I'm also a woman."

A woman who obviously had made some decisions in her past based on needs other than her own—decisions she apparently regretted now.

Elise held out her hand for Lilly, wanting to offer comfort to her, but the older woman was already reaching for the curtain. Maybe someone had called out to her, because she rushed away without another word, leaving Elise reeling from what she'd said or rather what she'd left unsaid.

Lilly had just offered Elise more support than even her own mother would have in this situation. Her mother would urge her to tell Neil, to let him be involved in his child's life. Although, that was because Elise's own father had abandoned them, and Aubrey Willis knew how hard being a single mother was.

Elise knew, too, because of all her mother had sacrificed for her. She didn't want to make those kinds of sacrifices; that was why she hadn't been in a rush to start a family, like Neil had been.

He deserved to know, though, that he was finally going to get his wish. He was going to be a father.

They must be in shock...

Neither Neil nor Elise had spoken since walking through the door of the room that the head nurse—aka Mom—had provided for the police interview. While the head nurse had refused to comment on their medical conditions, Mom had revealed that they were being released. So they hadn't been seriously hurt in the explosion.

Once she'd learned that, Jordana had assured Clint that he could leave the hospital. Reese, her partner, would drop her home when they took a break in their investigation for the night.

"Are you both really all right?" she asked again. Those had been her first words when each had walked into the room just seconds ago. In reply, all she'd received were head nods. Well, actually just a head nod from Elise. Neil had been too busy studying his ex-wife's face to do even that.

This time he did. But that was all he did. He remained silent, just like Elise—which was so totally out of character for the lawyers who rarely stopped talking or arguing. Concern gripped Jordana. Were they really all right?

"We need you to answer our questions," Reese said, irritation making his voice gruff. "We need to know what the hell happened tonight."

Neil shrugged. "I don't know."

And Jordana wondered if he was talking about the explosion or something else—something that had him staring so intensely at Elise that her own heart ached over the look of longing on her brother's face.

Like her brother, she focused on her ex-sister-in-law. "Why did you ask Neil to meet you at the warehouse?" she asked.

Elise shook her head now. "I didn't."

Jordana's brow furrowed and she turned to her brother. "You told me that—"

"I got a message that was supposed to be from her," he said. "But it wasn't."

"And I got the same from him," Elise said, "asking me to meet him there."

"A setup," Reese said.

"The explosion wasn't an accident, then," Jordana said. Neither was Neil and Elise being there at the exact time of the blast.

"Did you see anyone?" Reese asked.

They both shook their heads this time.

"No sign of Markus Dexter?" he asked.

"No," Neil said. "What about you? Do you have any idea where he is?"

Jordana shook her head. "No. Ever since we served a search warrant on his house, there's been a unit sitting on it, watching it to see if either he or his wife returns. The evidence is still being processed from the search. But so far there have been no clues to lead us to where he's gone."

"He must not have gone far," Reese remarked.

"You think he was behind the explosion?" Elise asked. "But why would he try to hurt me and Neil?"

Reese shrugged now. "You're not the only Colton he tried killing recently."

Jordana flinched with a twinge of pain and fear over how the family could have lost Ty when Dexter had shot him. He was pretty much fully recovered, though— albeit more from love than medicine, probably. Like her, her brother had recently found love, too.

She could only hope that her relationship fared better than Neil and Elise's had.

"I'm not a Colton," Elise said. "So it doesn't make sense for him to try to kill me."

"Maybe he blames you for the bodies being discovered—because of your plans for the city," Jordana suggested.

"I guess he wouldn't be the only one to have problems with my politics," Elise admitted.

A smile tugged at Jordana's lips. Her father had made it clear what he thought of Elise's plans to continue her predecessor's policy of limiting urban sprawl. Not damn much…

"We really don't know anything to help with your investigation," Neil said, and now irritation was making his voice gravelly. "It's late. If we think of anything else, we'll let you know."

"We need those messages that lured you both to the warehouse," Reese said.

"My assistant received a call from who she thought was someone in Neil's office," Elise said.

"Same here," Neil added.

"Then we'll need to talk to your assistants," Reese said.

"In the morning," Jordana told her partner. She wanted to get back to her house and to Clint. He'd come down early for a long weekend. Unfortunately, she still had to work tomorrow, since it was Friday.

"We don't have anything else to tell you, so we're going to leave now," Neil informed them. Without waiting for the interview to officially end, he clasped Elise's arm and escorted her toward the door.

A strange look of dread and resignation crossed

Elise's beautiful face. She obviously didn't want to leave with Neil. Of course, most women didn't want to hang out with their ex-husbands, but Elise wasn't most women. She and Neil were that rare couple who'd managed to maintain a friendship even after their divorce.

So what was going on with them?

"What the hell?" Reese asked after the door closed. "Why'd you let them walk out of here?"

Jordana sighed. "I know them." And how damn stubborn they both were. "They're not going to answer any more questions tonight."

Reese shook his head, mussing up his already mussed-up, overly long hair. "It's crazy. If someone tried to kill me, I'd be the one asking the questions. I'd be so damn mad...unless..."

"Unless what?" Jordana asked.

"I know they were married before, so was this some kind of murder-suicide thing? One of them trying to take out the other?"

Jordana gasped with shock, then laughed. Like her, Reese had been a detective too long—so long that he'd grown cynical. "That's crazy."

"He's your brother, so of course you'd have trouble suspecting him."

"And you suspect everyone of everything," she admonished him. "I know them both, and they're not murderous or suicidal. They've been divorced a few years, with no animosity between them."

"I'm not so sure about that," Reese said. "I could feel the tension in this room. Something's going on with them."

Jordana couldn't laugh off that suspicion. She'd suspected the same damn thing.

"They're keeping something from us," Reese said.

She nodded in agreement. "But it might not have anything to do with what happened tonight."

And everything to do with the two of them.

"Whatever it is, we need to know," he said. "And they need to know that their lives are at risk."

Jordana sucked in a breath of fear for her brother. Her partner, however cynical, was right. Neil was in danger and maybe not just from whoever had caused the explosion.

"We're in serious trouble," Neil told Elise, his stomach knotting at the thought of how bad the threat was. They could have been killed earlier. And if they had…

He nearly choked on the emotion rushing over him. "We need to get out of here."

What if whoever had set them up had followed the ambulance to the hospital? Neil suspected he might have, because once they stepped out the doors of the hospital, that sensation rushed over him again—of someone watching him.

It could have been Jordana and her partner, though. Detective Carpenter obviously hadn't wanted to end the interview when Neil had. But the detectives weren't who either he or Elise needed to talk to at the moment.

They needed to talk to each other. He had so damn many questions for her. One more important than any other.

"How are we getting out of here?" Elise asked.

"Our vehicles are back at the warehouse and might be burned up."

He held up a key fob. "My mother loaned me hers."

Elise expelled a ragged sigh. "Good. Then you can drop me home."

"I'm taking you home," Neil said. To the house they'd designed together. The one they had intended to share for the rest of their lives. The one Neil had wanted to fill with children...

He clicked the fob, and the lights flashed on his mom's vehicle. Hastening his step, he made it to the passenger's door before her and pulled it open. But she didn't slide onto the seat. Instead, she just stood and stared at him.

"I want to go to my place," she said.

"The security is better at mine," he said. His brother, Tyler, being a security expert, Neil had the best alarm system on the market. That wasn't the only reason he wanted Elise to come home with him, though. "And we need to talk..."

"We can do that here," she said.

That strange sensation—of being watched—continued to chill his flesh, though, and he shook his head. "Not here."

She sighed. "What's to talk about, Neil? You know I'm pregnant."

A sharp pain jabbed his heart. "You are?"

She nodded. "Yes, I am. And as I told your sister, I'm fine. I am also exhausted, so talking about anything else can wait until tomorrow."

"This can't," he insisted.

"What?"

"My proposal," he said.

She sighed again, clearly getting frustrated with him. "What do you propose, Neil?"

"That you marry me."

Chapter 5

"Did you hit your head?" Elise asked. Again. She'd asked that the moment Neil had proposed to her in the hospital parking lot.

He'd claimed he was fine. But suspecting that he had a concussion, she'd agreed to go back to the house with him and also because she had the same uneasy feeling he had, that they were being watched.

Maybe someone had been watching. Or maybe they were just being overly cautious after what had nearly happened to them. They'd nearly been killed.

Would have been if not for Neil's quick thinking. She owed him for saving her life, but becoming his wife wasn't the correct way to repay him. They'd tried that already. He'd been the one to end it—to end their marriage.

But that was because…

She pressed her hand against her stomach. It was still flat, or as flat as it ever was, since she never had the time or the inclination to work out. He had either proposed because she was pregnant or because he was concussed. Maybe both.

He hadn't forgotten the code to the security system at the front door, though. He punched in the number—the date he'd originally proposed to her—and the red light flashed to green on the console. Closing the door, he glanced around the darkened foyer as if looking for someone hiding in the shadows.

"You said it's the best security system," she reminded him. And she doubted anyone could have guessed the passcode. Nobody else knew how soon he'd proposed after their first meeting in that law school lecture hall.

He poked his head in the door off the foyer, to the den, before heading cautiously past the stairwell toward the open area at the back of the house, which combined the kitchen and great room. As he walked, he flipped on all the lights.

"I'm sure nobody got inside," she assured him as she peered around the space. "Not even a decorator…"

"Decorator?" he echoed the word, finally seeming to emerge from the coma he'd been in since the explosion, or at least since she'd told the paramedic she might be pregnant. "The house looks the same as it did when you lived here."

They had decorated it together, just as they'd designed it. They'd picked out every cabinet, every paint color. That was why she hadn't wanted it in the divorce, but she hadn't been surprised that he had. Obviously he hadn't been as sentimental as she was, or he wouldn't have filed for divorce in the first place.

"You haven't decorated for Christmas yet," she said, clarifying her remark, as she pointed toward the empty space in front of the tall windows where they'd put the tree in the past.

"It's barely December," he said.

Braxville had put up the twinkling lights and wreaths in the town square even before Thanksgiving. She'd thought the tradition a bit premature, but after she became mayor, she didn't dare discontinue it. To do so would cost her votes in the next election. Would being a single mother also cost her votes?

Not that she would ever consider accepting Neil's proposal, even if he was serious.

But he couldn't be serious.

"See, I remember what month it is," he said. "I don't have a concussion. What about you?"

Maybe she had hit her head; it would explain why she'd come back here again, especially after what had happened the last time she'd come home with him.

She moved her hand over her stomach and sighed. "I told you I was fine," she said. He could have found out for himself if he'd really wanted to know. She hadn't removed him as her next of kin or durable medical power of attorney. She had no one else in Braxville.

Her mother lived in Detroit, Michigan, where Elise had been born and raised. She might have returned there after law school if she hadn't met and fallen so hard for Neil that she'd moved to his hometown.

"What you said earlier…" His hand covered hers on her stomach. "You really are…?" His voice trailed off as if he couldn't utter the word, as if he didn't dare believe it was possible.

"Pregnant?" She nodded.

"That's why you need to marry me," he said.

She snorted. "You might not have hit your head, but you've lost your damn mind. I am not marrying you."

"But you're pregnant."

"And this isn't 1920," she said. "I can be a single mom." Not that doing so was something she had ever planned.

In fact, that would have been the last damn thing she ever planned on being, after watching her mom struggle so much to raise Elise on her own.

"But you don't want to be a single mom," he said.

Damn it.

He knew her too well. Sometimes.

Other times it was as if he'd never known her at all.

"I'm not going to marry you," she said. Not because of the baby.

Now, if he loved her—just her—she might have been tempted to accept. But he'd never really loved just her, or he wouldn't have divorced her in the first place.

Tears stung her eyes, but she blinked them back. Damn hormones. She never cried. Not even when she'd received those divorce papers.

Neil must have noticed her struggle with emotion because he reached out, cupping her cheek in his palm. "Are you really okay?"

She nodded. "Yes, the blood work confirmed the

pregnancy. And although it's too soon to see much of anything, the doctor also confirmed that I didn't miscarry. That everything looks fine."

"Are *you* fine?" he asked.

No. Not now.

Not with him staring at her so intently, touching her so gently.

"What's wrong?" he asked.

Neil's stomach clenched, knots forming as he gazed at the tears shimmering in Elise's green eyes. She never cried. Not even when he'd told her that he couldn't stay married to her. If she had, he might have known that she cared, that she loved him as much as he loved her. But she'd given him no indication that it mattered to her whether they were married or not.

She was giving him a clear indication now that she had no intention of accepting his proposal, though, of ever being his wife again. So obviously she preferred their divorce over their marriage.

She blinked, her lashes fluttering over those green-green eyes. "What do you think is wrong?"

He didn't want to believe that she was upset about being pregnant, that she regretted that night they'd spent together a month ago.

Fortunately, she answered her own question. "We could have been killed tonight," she said, her voice cracking with emotion. "If you hadn't gotten us out of there when you did."

"I should have realized right away that it was a setup," he admonished himself. "I should have gotten us out of there sooner." Hell, he never should have let her walk into the warehouse.

Not only was it a crime scene but it could potentially pose health risks if Bridgette was right, if the buildings Colton Construction had renovated were somehow contaminated.

"Are you sure you're okay?" he asked again. "That the doctors thoroughly checked you out?"

"I'm fine," she assured him. "I'm just tired and overwhelmed."

It was late. And they'd been through so much that evening. Now was not the time to press her to accept his proposal, if he could even come up with an argument that could convince her. He moved his hand from her face, and then he swung her up in his arms.

She clutched at his shoulders. "What are you doing?" she asked.

"Bringing you to bed," he said as he carried her through the great room to the double doors on the other side of it. He'd left them ajar that morning, so he was able to push easily through them to the master bedroom. The bed was unmade, the sheets rumpled from his restless sleep the night before. Next to the four-poster bed, he released her, letting her soft, curvy body slide down his.

"I should sleep in one of the guest bedrooms," she said. But she made no move toward the doors.

She might need to be with him as much as he needed to be with her. He could have lost her tonight. Could have lost *them*…without ever knowing that they'd conceived a child together. The child he'd wanted so badly.

Emotion rushed over him now. "Please," he implored her. "Marry me again, Elise."

"Why?" she asked.

Because he never should have divorced her in the first place. He'd been such a fool. So stubborn…

He realized that now. Hell, he'd realized that then. But as well as stubborn, he was proud—like his father. Too proud to admit to all the mistakes he'd made.

"Last month you told me that you weren't seeing anyone else," he reminded her. "So this baby is mine. I want him or her to have my name."

"What's wrong with my name?" she asked. "Isn't Willis as good as Colton?"

"Right now, being a Willis is probably better," he assured her.

Nobody in Braxville was happy with his father right now. While Fitz Colton might not have known about his partner allegedly being a killer, why hadn't he done something about so many of his workers getting seriously sick? A couple had even died.

"And I'm fine if the baby has your name, too. But I want…"

Her.

She pressed her finger over his lips. "Shh…it's late, Neil, and I don't want to fight."

Neither did he. Unfortunately they did it entirely too often. Sometimes fighting with her—matching wits with her stimulating mind—was exhilarating. Other times—when she was as stubborn as he was and refused to concede defeat—fighting with her exhausted him.

And she had already admitted to being tired. He

wasn't going to push her tonight, not when he could see how determined she was. She wasn't going to give him a win and let him put her ring back on her finger. Not tonight.

"Let's just go to bed," he suggested, and he flicked his tongue across the finger she held over his lips.

She shivered and murmured, "Neil..."

"We're alive, Elise," he reminded her. Despite someone's effort to end their lives. "Let's celebrate that tonight." And that they were having a child—whether they had decided to have it together or apart.

He pushed that horrible thought from his mind, though. He would come up with a better argument. He would eventually convince her to marry him again. He couldn't live without her. If something had happened to her tonight...

He shuddered and closed his arms around her. She stood for a moment in the circle of them, her body tense. Then she slid her arms around his waist and clutched him tightly. Like the hug at her car a month ago, passion ignited over the closeness of their bodies.

Hers so curvy and soft. His so hard he ached with tension, with need...for her. After nearly losing her tonight, he had to be close to her again—part of her again.

She must have felt the same desire, because she moved her arms from his waist to his neck and pulled his head down to hers. She kissed him passionately, hungrily. Like she had the night they'd conceived their baby. Remembering that, remembering what they'd been through, he pulled back. "Are you sure it's safe to do this?"

She chuckled. "I'm already pregnant."

"That's what I mean," he said. "We're not going to hurt the baby?"

She shook her head, but she studied his face for a moment…like she was looking for something. She had to see how much he wanted her, how much he always wanted her. And in case she didn't see it, he showed her.

He leaned down and kissed her back with all the passion he felt for her. And as he kissed her, he pushed her coat from her shoulders. He needed nothing between his skin and hers. She must have felt the same, because she dealt with his buttons and zippers with as much impatience as he showed in tackling hers…until they stood naked before each other.

No. They weren't entirely naked. There were always thin walls between them, holding them apart. He knew it. Some of those walls were his, his way of avoiding getting hurt. Were hers the same?

Was that why she'd turned down his proposal? She didn't trust him again.

With her heart…

She trusted him with her body. So he made sure to give her pleasure. Gently tugging her onto the rumpled bed, he made love to her with his hands and his mouth before she pulled him down on top of her. She guided him inside, joining their bodies.

He moved slowly…until she began to move beneath him. She knew just what to do, how to move, where to touch him, kiss him…so that he lost control and found his release, his mind-blowing release.

Despite the pleasure they'd given each other, though,

his body was still tense, his mind unable to shut off the flow of all his concerns. All he could do was hold her tightly against him and try to keep her safe through the night…but he worried that someone was out there, waiting to try for them again.

His cell phone vibrated across the surface of his nightstand, and a groan slipped out of Ty Colton's mouth. He ran his hand over his head, mussing his dark brown hair. It was getting too long, starting to curl too much.

"What?" a soft voice murmured as Ashley shifted against his side. Her silky dark hair fell over his arm as she snuggled closer to him.

Love warmed his heart, making it swell in his chest. Ashley Hart was such an incredible woman. A socialite. A philanthropist. A freaking genius. Not to mention drop-dead gorgeous.

It made total sense that he'd fallen for her after he'd been hired to protect her. But that she'd fallen for him, too…

How had he gotten so lucky?

The phone continued to vibrate, drawing his attention back to it and another groan from his throat.

"Nobody ever calls at this hour with good news…" Not that he was entirely sure what time it was. They'd been eating dinner and she'd looked so damn beautiful that he'd wanted her instead. Tempted to ignore the call and focus on Ashley, Ty groaned again into the cell phone as he swiped his hand across the screen.

"Are you okay?" his sister asked, Jordana's voice gruff with concern.

"Yeah," he said.

"But you're groaning," she said. "Is your gunshot wound bothering you?"

"The only thing bothering me is someone interrupting my sleep," he said. "What's going on?"

"You need to come home."

"I am home." Never more so than now, since Ashley had moved in with him.

"You're in Wichita," she said. "You need to be here in Braxville."

He sighed. "I'm a security expert, Jord. I'm safe here. And I doubt Markus Dexter will try to get to me again."

"He might have tried getting to Neil tonight."

He cursed and jolted upright in bed. "Has Neil been shot? Is he okay?"

Ashley sat up next to him, her big brown eyes even wider with concern.

"He was nearly blown up," his sister said, her voice shaking with emotion. "But he got out of the building in time. The bomb was set at the warehouse where the bodies were discovered."

He sucked in a breath.

"Is Neil okay?" Ashley asked.

He nodded but repeated the question to Jordana.

"Yes, he's fine. But he shouldn't have been there."

"What the hell was he doing there?" Ty asked. "He has nothing to do with the investigation, nothing to do with Colton Construction. Unless…" A horrible thought occurred to him, but he shook it off. Neil was a criminal lawyer, but he was too loyal to his family to ever represent the man who'd tried to kill Tyler.

"Unless what?" Jordana asked.

"Nothing. What was he doing there?"

"He thought Elise wanted to meet him there."

Ty cursed again. "Of course." And for some reason, despite divorcing her, his brother could not stay away from his ex-wife.

"She thought the same," Jordana continued. "It was a setup."

"It would make more sense that the mayor would be the target," Ty said. "Maybe Dexter blames her campaign against urban sprawl for those bodies being discovered."

"So you think Dexter killed those people?"

"Don't you?" Ty asked. "One of them was probably his mistress, since he's been rumored to have many. And the other body was the private investigator trying to find her after she was murdered. How can you not think Dexter killed them?"

"I'm waiting for conclusive evidence," the detective maintained.

Ty snorted. "Yeah, right. Has any been found?"

"His house was searched—"

"Bet his wife loved that," Ty remarked.

"She'd already left town."

"Alone?"

"Don't think she wants anything to do with her husband or the scandal, but we have a unit watching the house in case anyone comes back. Nobody has come back yet."

"That you've seen," Ty said. "But who else besides Dexter would want to blow up that warehouse?"

"Since they were lured there with those messages, Neil and Elise might have been the targets more than Crest View Center. That's why you need to come home. You need to help me keep Neil safe."

"Of course," Ty agreed.

He could protect his brother from whomever had set that bomb, but who would protect Neil from his ex-wife? Ty had a feeling that Neil's life wasn't the only thing in danger; his heart was, too.

Chapter 6

What the hell did I just do?

Her body answered that question. Limp with sexual satisfaction, Elise nearly melted into the tangled sheets. Maybe it was the hormones that had had her reacting so passionately to Neil's kiss. Or maybe it had been their close brush with death that had heightened all her senses.

But what had been her excuse a month ago when she'd gotten pregnant? At least that couldn't happen again. She was already as pregnant as she was going to get.

She pressed her hand over her stomach but felt nothing until Neil's hand slid over hers. Then her skin tingled, and her pulse leaped. Even after what they'd just done, how much pleasure he'd just given her, she wanted him again.

Damn hormones.

"Are you really all right?" he asked.

"Me?" she asked. "Or the baby?" That was whom he was really concerned about, the only reason he wanted to marry her.

"Both of you," he said. "I could have lost you tonight."

"Last night," she murmured, as she glanced at the clock beside the bed. She corrected him about the time but not about the fact that he didn't have her, that he hadn't had her since he'd divorced her.

Even that night...

It had been a lapse, a slipup. It had been passion, not love. He couldn't have ended their marriage if he'd really loved her.

"You need to rest," he said. "Especially now."

Now that she carried his child. In the past she'd worried about losing herself to him. That was why she hadn't fought the divorce. She'd known then that he hadn't been with her for her but for the life they could build together: the life he'd wanted, the law practice, the kids...his family.

She gasped as she felt now like she'd felt then, like she was drowning under all the expectations, of all the responsibilities of being a Colton.

"What is it?" he asked. "Are you all right? Did you feel the baby move?"

"No. Although the doctor assured me everything was

normal, I couldn't even see anything on the ultrasound, so I doubt I'll feel anything for a while."

"Oh…" he murmured with clear disappointment. Then he clutched her hand in his, entwining their fingers. "I want to be there when you have the next ultrasound. I want to be there when you first feel the baby move. I want to be there for you during this pregnancy, Elise. Please marry me again."

She closed her eyes against the tears rushing to them. "Neil…"

"You don't have to do this alone, like your mother did," he persisted.

She cursed. How could he know her so well in some regards and so little in others? He knew how she'd felt about the struggle her mother had had raising Elise on her own, but he didn't fully grasp how that had affected her.

"I will be there for you," he vowed, "if you'll let me."

No. He would be there for the baby and that baby was the only reason he would be with her. She wanted more. She deserved more.

"I am not my mother," she said through gritted teeth. "I will be fine."

"You don't know that," he said. "Not after what happened."

Making love with him or the explosion?

A ragged sigh slipped through her lips. "What the hell did happen?" she wondered and not just to her common sense but in the warehouse. "It doesn't make sense."

None of it made sense. Making love with him and

someone trying to kill them. The explosion could have been an accident, another side effect of some of the faulty construction that had gone on in Braxville. But why had someone lured them both there?

"We'll figure it all out in the morning," he said. "You need to rest now."

With all the thoughts and fears swirling through her head, she wasn't sure she would be able to sleep. But she intended to pretend that she was…just until he fell asleep. Then she would be able to leave without an argument. Without another proposal.

Without any temptation to accept that proposal and stay with him forever.

No. She needed to get the hell out of there before she did anything else crazy, like falling in love with him all over again. But even as she resolved to stay awake, her lids began to droop over eyes gritty from exhaustion and maybe debris from the explosion.

It had to have been accident. Somebody couldn't really be trying to kill them. Could he?

She was gone. Neil knew it before he even opened his eyes—because he was cold, his skin chilled by the loss of her warmth, her presence.

Damn.

He shouldn't have fallen asleep again, shouldn't have risked her leaving without him. Not when she was in so much danger.

Something creaked and the security system alarm sounded. Maybe she wasn't gone yet or maybe someone had broken into the house.

He jerked fully awake and jumped out of the bed. The minute his feet hit the floor, he ran for the front door where the alarm control panel was. But the high-pitched siren cut out, as someone pushed the buttons for the security code.

"Elise…"

He'd caught her trying to sneak out, just as he'd suspected she might. He shouldn't have fallen asleep, but she must have, as well, because the sun was high and bright, casting a glow through the front door that shimmered in her golden hair.

She sighed, and her shoulders slumped as if defeated over being caught. "I don't want to fight," she said before she looked away from the panel to focus on his face.

Dark circles rimmed her green eyes, making it clear she hadn't slept, or at least not enough that she was rested.

"I don't want to fight, either," he said. "I just want to make sure you're safe."

"I'm fine," she said. "And I need to get to work."

"You don't have a car," he reminded her. "And I need to get my mother's car back to her."

She sighed. "I'll call a cab. I need to go home first and change before going into the office anyway."

His skin chilled, reminding him that he hadn't bothered to dress when he'd run out of his bedroom at the sound of his alarm. At least, sometime during the night, he must have pulled his boxers back on, though. He wasn't as physically cold as he was emotionally—at the thought of her running around town without protection.

"Before I return my mother's car," he said, "I'll take you to your condo and then to the office."

She grimaced. "You don't need to do that. I'm not helpless."

"No, you're not," he agreed. "But you are in danger."

She shook her head. "I don't think so."

"That building blew up—"

"It could have been an accident," she said. "More faulty construction."

"And it was just a coincidence that it blew up after fake messages lured us both there?" he asked, shaking his head now. "You don't really believe that any more than I do."

She narrowed her eyes and glared at him. "It doesn't matter what happened or why. It and you are not going to stop me from doing my job."

"I don't want to stop you," he assured her. He knew how much her job meant to her. "I just want to make sure you're safe when you're working."

She sighed again, but this time it sounded as if it was with resignation. "Okay, but you might want to get dressed first."

Suspicious of her sudden agreement, he narrowed his eyes and studied her beautiful face. Was she going to run out of the house the minute he went back to the bedroom to dress? He wouldn't put it past her.

"Elise, I know you're anxious to get to work, but I hope you're taking this threat seriously. You could have been killed."

Her hand pressed against her flat stomach. And he knew she wasn't thinking just of herself anymore. "I'll wait for you," she promised. "You can even shower if you want…"

He wanted her—in the shower with him—water sluicing over her naked skin. "You need to shower, too," he said as he stepped closer to her so their bodies just brushed. She had on too damn many clothes now, her jacket over her black slacks and heavy sweater. He wanted—*needed*—her naked again. "Want to join me?"

Her pupils dilated, swallowing the green irises, but she shook her head even as her lips curved into a slight smile. "You need to get to work, too."

She was right. He needed to get to work—not at his office, though. He wasn't currently representing anyone. He needed to get to work finding out who had left those messages for them—who had tried to kill them.

And he had to make sure that person didn't get the chance to try again.

Yvette Colton stared at the blackened shell of the warehouse from which she'd collected evidence months ago. If she'd missed anything then, it was probably gone now. Had that been the purpose of this explosion?

Or had it been an accident?

The sun had risen over what remained of the warehouse while she waited in the parking lot for the fire department to deem it safe enough for her to enter the structure. Their arson inspector hadn't had to wait like she had, though.

He walked out now, and as he ducked under the yellow tape, she rushed up to meet him. He was an older man, older probably even than her father and Uncle

Shep, because his hair was completely gray and his face was lined with age.

"So?" she asked. "What do you think?"

"You don't need to go in," he said, and he held up a bag. "I got what you're looking for."

"What is it?" she asked, trying to visually examine the contents through the plastic, since he still held tightly to the bag.

"Incendiary device," he said.

"So it wasn't an accident."

"Nope. Looks like the type that had to be detonated. You might find that out here," he said as he glanced around the lot. "I was told there was nobody inside the building when it exploded, so no casualties, fortunately. But if nobody was inside, whose vehicles are these?"

Like the warehouse, the little hybrid coupe was a blackened shell of what it had formerly been. The plate, though, was intact enough that a detective had made out the raised letters and numbers in the metal and run them through the department of motor vehicles.

"That's the mayor's," she said.

"And that one?" He pointed toward the SUV parked farther from the building. It had a fine sheen of soot on it and some debris, but it wasn't burned up like the hybrid.

If it had been closer, though…

If he had been closer…

Yvette's heart did a little flip in her chest as fear and panic rushed over her again. She knew he was okay; Jordana had assured her of that. But it could have been so much worse. "My brother's."

"The security guy?" the inspector asked.

"Not Tyler. Neil, the lawyer," she replied.

He chuckled. "Not surprised someone might have tried to kill a lawyer."

She was. Even though people often made derogatory remarks about lawyers, especially those who practiced criminal law like Neil, she hadn't thought anyone would actually act on that prejudice. And she couldn't believe that now.

Was Markus Dexter involved, like he'd been with Ty's shooting? Was her father's friend and business partner going to go after all of them?

She found it hard to imagine that he'd risk coming back to town now—with an outstanding warrant for his arrest.

No. More than likely this attempt had been personal.

Had Neil ticked someone off? Someone other than Elise?

Her cell vibrated inside her pocket, startling her. She quickly pulled it out and glanced at the screen. "It's Neil calling me now," she said.

"Tell him to be careful," the arson investigator advised. "He and the mayor got damn lucky this time. They might not be that lucky the next time."

The next...

If someone had meant to kill Neil or Elise, they probably wouldn't give up after one failed attempt.

Chapter 7

Someone had tried to kill them.

Elise had known that the second the warehouse had exploded, but she hadn't wanted to admit it, even to herself. Because then she would have had to accept that Neil was right to be so overprotective of her.

He'd insisted on driving her back to her condo and waiting while she showered and changed. When she was getting ready, she'd heard the rumble of his voice as he spoke to someone on his cell. She'd thought he might have been checking in with his office, but when she joined him in the living room, he'd told her to pack a suitcase.

"Why?" she asked, glancing around her condo. Had something happened while she was in the bathroom?

"You need to stay with me," he said. "My house is safer than this place."

She didn't have the high-tech alarm system he did, but with curious and concerned neighbors close, she'd always felt safe in the complex. "You're overreacting," she told him.

But he shook his head. "The arson investigator confirmed that was a bomb in the warehouse, one that someone detonated thinking we were still inside."

"You called the arson investigator?" she asked.

He shook his head. "No, my sister."

"Jordana knows more than she did last night, then," Elise mused.

"Yvette," he said, identifying his youngest sister, the CSI. "She's processing evidence from the crime scene and was with the arson investigator when I called. So there is no doubt that someone tried to kill us last night."

Her knees trembled a bit, but she locked her legs, refusing to give in to the fear that crashed over her. She would not let what happened weaken her.

"What else did your sister say?" she asked.

Hopefully, Yvette had found evidence that would help identify the bomber.

"You're going to need a new car," Neil said.

Tempted to curse, she chuckled instead. With her life being threatened, the car was the very least of her concerns at the moment, so she quipped, "Now you know what to get me for Christmas."

"You know what I want to get you," he said as he reached out for her hand. "A diamond ring."

"Neil…" She pulled her hand free of his, but her skin tingled yet from even that brief contact.

"Come on, Elise, look at this place." He gestured at the close confines of her townhome-style condo. "You can't raise a baby here."

"I can if I want," she said. "They don't take up much room." In the beginning…

"I have more than enough room," he said. "We built that house for our future family."

"You did," she said. "I thought we were building it for us." But she hadn't been enough to make him happy. He'd wanted more.

"We did build it for us," he said. "Move back in with me. Marry me."

That curse slipped out now. "Neil, you have to stop. This isn't an argument you're going to win. And I don't have time for you to keep trying." She glanced at the thin gold watch on her wrist. Her mother had saved and saved to be able to buy it for her for her college graduation. "I need to get to the office before word gets out about what happened last night."

"That you were nearly killed." He shuddered, and his blue eyes gleamed with emotion. "Elise…"

She felt the same way. No matter what had happened between them, no matter that she wouldn't accept his proposal, she couldn't imagine a world without him in it. "I know."

"So will you pack a bag?" he asked. "Will you come home with me tonight?"

"I want to talk to Jordana and that other detective

first," she said. "I want to know how the investigation is going. Maybe they've found Markus Dexter."

"I'm not so sure it was Markus Dexter who tried to kill us," Neil said.

"Who else would it be?" she wondered.

He shrugged. "I don't know."

"It has to be him," she persisted. "Obviously he has access to explosives since he was in the construction business with your father."

"But it makes no sense for him to come after us." He ran a hand over his head, mussing his thick brown hair. "We'll figure it out. But until we do, you need to be safe, so you'll stay with me."

"I have to get to work," she said as she jerked open her door and stepped outside.

He must have finally realized he wasn't going to win this argument, either, because he followed her out and locked the door behind them. Then he clicked the fob for his mother's vehicle and opened the passenger's door for her.

"What about your SUV?" she asked. "Did it survive the explosion?"

A slight grin curved his lips. "I parked far enough away from the building that it's fine."

She glared at him because she suspected he was teasing her for her penchant of finding the closest parking spot in order to avoid a long walk to whatever business she was patronizing. Parking close was convenient in case she had a lot to carry out to her car.

It hadn't been convenient in this case, though. She

hated car shopping, but at least she was alive to do it. And Neil was alive, too.

He chuckled as he closed her door. Then he walked around to the driver's side and slid behind the wheel. "You might be safer with your vehicle out of commission."

"Are you calling me a bad driver?" she asked, anger beginning to bubble up. Didn't he think she could do anything right or at least on her own? His overprotectiveness had been another issue in their marriage, his wanting to take care of her.

In the beginning she'd thought it was sweet that he hadn't let her be alone with any of their clients who'd been accused of abusive behavior. Eventually it had worn on her that he hadn't treated her as an equal. She'd just wanted him to trust her to take care of herself.

"No," he said. "I meant that whoever is after us won't be able to put a bomb in your car." He hesitated for a moment before turning the key in the ignition, as if worried that someone had put a bomb on this one.

But this was his mother's vehicle, not his.

"I still need to have a car," she said.

"Maybe you should wait until we find out who lured us to the warehouse."

"Has to be Dexter," she said.

"Why?" he asked. "Because you prefer to think that he's the only criminal in Braxville?"

"I know better than that," she said. From the years she'd been his partner in their criminal law practice, as well as from her time in the mayor's office. While Braxville had far less crime than where she'd grown up in Detroit, it wasn't entirely safe—as last night had proved.

City Hall wasn't far from her condo, so they pulled up in front of the building in just minutes. They weren't the only ones arriving at the scene; news vehicles had lined up along the curb. Neil was lucky to find a spot at one of the meters, and she wasn't even concerned it was just a two-hour meter. She didn't want him staying to babysit her.

And she definitely didn't want the reporters seeing them arrive together. She groaned. "Word must have gotten out about last night." She'd hoped it wouldn't have, at least not until a suspect had been apprehended.

"Want me to drive you around to a rear entrance so you can avoid them?" he asked.

She shook her head. "No. I better deal with this right away."

"Are you going to address your pregnancy, too?" he asked.

"Why?" she asked. "I'm still in the first trimester. There's a chance…"

He gasped. "That you could lose the baby? But I thought everything was okay?"

She found herself reaching across the console to grasp his hand, to reassure him. "That's what the doctor said, but things can happen at any time, just like us nearly getting blown up last night."

"That's why you need to stay with me," he persisted. "Why you need to marry me…"

She groaned. "I'm not going to discuss this pregnancy with the reporters or with you anymore until you stop spontaneously proposing to me."

Before he could continue arguing with her, she pushed open the car door and stepped onto the sidewalk. She'd only made it a short distance from the vehicle before a reporter spotted her. Then they all swarmed like shoppers over Black Friday specials.

An unfamiliar sensation rushed over her, making her pulse quicken with anxiety. She had never minded talking to reporters before. But maybe it was because of what had happened last night, and the uncertainty whether it would happen again, that made her uneasy.

Someone had tried to kill her and Neil. And now, knowing he or she hadn't succeeded, that person was bound to try again.

Neil couldn't leave Elise unprotected, so he jumped out of his mother's car, fed some coins into the meter and joined the reporters on the sidewalk. Anger tightened his stomach muscles as he listened to them bombard Elise with questions without giving her a second to answer any of them.

"Mayor, was there an attempt on your life?"

"Do you know who's responsible?"

"Were you seriously injured?"

"Were you alone at the time of the attack?"

"Will you be able to continue your duties as mayor?"

He was just lifting his fingers to his lips when a whistle rent the air and silenced the reporters. He chuckled at Elise's tactic to gain their attention, one that an old law professor of theirs had used to silence an un-ruly class or to end an argument between him and Elise.

"Apparently, you've all learned that I was at the scene of the Crest View Center warehouse explosion last night," she began.

The reporters started speaking again, not giving her a chance to continue. But before Neil could step in, she let out another ear-piercing whistle.

"Last chance," she warned them. "I'm going to make a short statement before I get back to work. My state-ment will answer all the questions you need to have answered."

A grin tugged at Neil's lips. She was so damn tough and independent. So independent that she didn't need him. She never had.

He had been a fool to try to scare her about being a single parent like her mother. Nothing scared Elise. And he would make certain that even if they didn't get married again, she would not be raising their child all on her own like Aubrey Willis had raised Elise.

"The cause of the explosion last night is under in-vestigation, and out of respect for the Braxville Police Department, I will not comment on their open case," she said. "I will assure you all that I was not hurt, and I will not only be able to continue in my duties as mayor, but I will also be more focused on making sure that Braxville is safe for all our citizens."

The reporters began to speak again, but Elise turned away from them and headed up the steps to City Hall. She wore a long black coat, belted around her slim waist, over a sweater dress and tall black boots. She was so damn sexy.

He would have pushed through the reporters to follow her, but he suspected she would be irritated if the media realized they'd arrived together and that he was chasing after her. So he raised the collar of his jacket, tucked his head down and circled around to the back of the building. As he did, he glanced around to see if anyone had followed him or if anyone watched him like he and Elise had been last night.

Someone had waited until they'd gone inside the building before detonating the bomb, intending to kill them. Why?

It didn't make sense for Markus Dexter to come after them. They had nothing to do with the investigation into those murders.

But if not old Dex, who?

Who wanted them dead?

Anxious that he'd lost sight of Elise, Neil rushed to the back door. The security guard assigned to that entrance knew him, knew that he frequently visited the mayor, so he was allowed inside with only a cursory pat-down.

How safe was Elise here? Who else might be allowed up to see her without being thoroughly checked for weapons?

Maybe because of that cursory pat-down, Neil met Elise at the elevator bank. She'd gone through security in the main lobby and had probably had to answer questions from those guards about last night.

She sighed when she saw him. "I thought you left."

"Hoped," he surmised as the elevator doors opened.

She nodded as she stepped inside the car. "You need to stop being so overprotective. I'm in the building. It's secure. Nobody's going to get to me."

"I got to you," he said as he joined her inside the elevator.

She glared at him. "Because the guard at the back door knows you."

"He might know whoever set that bomb, too," Neil pointed out.

She sucked in a breath. "You really think it's someone who knows us?"

"Why else would someone lure us both to that warehouse?" he asked, hoping she might have some idea, because he didn't. But he would, once he gave his total attention to what had happened and not to what was going to happen.

He was going to be a father.

That news had hit him harder than the blast had knocked him to the ground. But in order to make sure he became a father, that his baby and the baby's mother lived, he needed to figure out who was behind that attack.

The elevator pinged as it arrived on the floor with her office. Her assistant jumped up the minute she saw Elise and rushed toward her. "Are you all right?" she asked. "When I saw the news this morning about the explosion and I knew you were meeting…" Her voice trailed off as she turned toward him, then her dark eyes narrowed with suspicion.

"I'm all right," Elise assured her. "And so is Neil."

"Why did you tell her to meet you there?" Carmen fired the question at him, but not as amiably as the reporters had questioned Elise.

"I didn't," he said. "You talked to the person who did. Was it a man or woman?"

Carmen pursed her lips as if searching her memory. Then she shrugged. "I don't know. It could have been a man or a woman with a raspy voice. She or he claimed to be leaving the message on your orders, though."

Neil shook his head. "Not mine. Nor did Elise leave the message that asked me to meet her at the warehouse."

Carmen gasped. "What the hell is going on?"

He shrugged but promised, "I'm going to find out."

"No, you're not. We're going to leave the investigation to the police." Elise turned to him as she said that, her green eyes narrowed like her aide's. "And you can leave me alone. I'm safe here." Without another word to either him or her assistant, she headed toward her office. But when she pushed open her door, she gasped.

Fear stabbed Neil's heart. Had a bomb been set up in her office? He rushed to her, edging around her in the doorway to confront whatever had shocked her. Someone sat in the chair behind her desk.

"What the hell," he murmured.

She edged him out of the way now as she pushed past him and walked to her desk. "Good morning, Jeremy, I see you've made yourself comfortable in my office. Unfortunately, the reports of my demise were greatly exaggerated."

The guy jumped up so quickly that her chair knocked

against the wall behind her desk. "Elise! Oh, thank God you're all right."

"No, thank Neil," she said.

Neil chuckled as the man, whose face had blanched white with shock, glanced at him. Well, he turned as white as he could with his artificial tan, which set off his blond hair and too-polished good looks.

"Uh, hi, Neil," Jeremy stammered. Usually the guy was a smooth talker, too smooth, but then he was a politician.

"Yeah, I'm alive, too," Neil informed him. "Hope you're not too disappointed."

"You were with her at the warehouse?" Jeremy asked. "The reports said her vehicle had been identified as the one destroyed at the scene."

"Mine survived," Neil said, "as did the two of us, which much have really upset whoever tried to kill us."

Jeremy gasped. "I—I can't imagine that was intentional," he said. "Elise is the most beloved mayor we've ever had."

Neil had always suspected Jeremy Lyons, her deputy mayor, was in love with her. But now he wondered…

At forty, Jeremy was ten years older than he and Elise were, and from his previous positions on the city council, he had more experience than she did. Was it Elise the man wanted, or was it her job? And what lengths would he go to in order to get what he wanted? Murder?

Attempted murder…

The attempted murder of the mayor. That was what

the reporters claimed had happened the night before, when the warehouse exploded.

He knew better.

It wasn't murder.

It was Justice.

And he was damn well going to get it.

Of course, it might be harder now. They would be expecting another attack. But maybe that was good. The bomb would have been quick, would have spared them the fear and misery they deserved to feel.

He wanted them to feel all the pain he'd felt.

So he moved his hands to the keyboard of the computer, and as he typed, the words appeared on the monitor in front of him.

He'll get what's coming to him.

Chapter 8

She'd gotten rid of Neil—after many assurances that she wouldn't leave the building or let into her office anyone that security hadn't thoroughly vetted. Before Neil had agreed to leave, he'd called down to security to make sure that Jeremy had come through the metal detectors at the front entrance of City Hall.

She was well aware that her ex-husband was not a fan of her deputy mayor, and vice versa. But to consider Jeremy capable of murder?

She couldn't, but...

He had been very quick to take her office. Carmen hadn't even realized that he'd been in it. So he must have arrived before her assistant had, but to do what? Check Elise's schedule as he'd claimed, so that if necessary, he would be able to fulfill her obligations?

How had he known that she might not be able to fulfill those obligations on her own? News reports about the explosion, and her possible presence at the site, hadn't leaked until the morning. So what had compelled him to come in so much earlier than he usually did?

How had he known something had happened to her? Or nearly happened…

She shivered as a chill rushed over her at how close they had come to dying. If Neil hadn't reacted as quickly as he had, they would both be dead. No. She pressed her hand over her stomach. They would all three be dead.

But why? Why would someone want to kill her and Neil at the same time?

If Jeremy wanted her job, he would only need to take out her, not her ex-husband, too. Unless he'd wanted it to look like something else. Like a murder-suicide so the case would be closed without much of an investigation. Maybe that was why the messages summoning them to the meeting had been made to look like they were from each other.

"Elise?"

Startled, she jumped in her chair, knocking it against the wall behind her like Jeremy had when she'd startled him earlier. The deputy mayor stood in the doorway, his handsome face tense with concern. For her? Or for himself?

"Are you all right?" he asked.

"Yes, I just didn't realize you were standing there," she said.

"I knocked," he claimed.

But it was a lie. She would have heard a knock. If he was lying about that, what else might he lie about?

"Do you need something?" she asked.

"No, just checking to see if you need anything," he replied solicitously. He'd been trying to ingratiate himself with her since she'd caught him in her office. He'd brought her coffee and doughnuts and asked her several times how he could help her. She didn't like all the groveling and fawning.

Maybe that was why she'd fallen for Neil. He wouldn't know how to do either. Although she'd once wished he did, after he'd served her divorce papers.

She'd wanted him to come to her and beg her forgiveness for making such a horrible mistake. But he hadn't.

And that had proved to her that the divorce wasn't a mistake. Marrying him again would be, though.

"Do you?" Jeremy asked. "Need anything?"

"A car," she quipped.

"I know a dealer," Jeremy said. "If you know what make and model you'd like, I could have him bring one to the office along with the paperwork."

"That would be helpful," she admitted. She really hated car shopping, but what she hated even more was relying on someone else to drive her where she wanted to go. Like Neil.

Before leaving her at the office earlier, he'd vowed he would return at the end of the day to take her home. He undoubtedly meant to his home.

She couldn't keep going back there, back to him.

"What kind of vehicle?" Jeremy asked. "Two-door, four-door?"

Less than a year from now, she would need a four-door—one with a back seat easily accessible for buckling in an infant carrier.

"Something safe," she replied. For herself and for her unborn child.

"I'll check the safety reports for you," Jeremy offered.

Those reports would tell him how well a vehicle would perform in a crash. But what about an explosion?

She needed to make sure that she wasn't at risk of one of those happening again. She needed to find out who the hell had lured her and Neil to that warehouse.

While she'd told Neil to leave the investigation to the police, she wasn't any more likely to do that than he was. She just wasn't sure where to start her inquiries.

With Jeremy?

Could he really want her office—her job—so badly that he would kill to take it?

He'll get what's coming to him.

The words were eerily familiar to Neil. He'd heard them before. But then, as a criminal lawyer, it would have been more surprising if he hadn't.

District attorneys said that. Victims said that. Police officers and detectives.

But who had said it this time? Who had sent him the strange email message? And was he the only one who'd received it?

He could have called Elise to ask her, but he'd wanted to see her again. Had needed to see her again…

To make sure she was all right, that she and the baby were safe.

Maybe she was—because security hadn't allowed him through the back door again. He'd had to use the front entrance with the metal detector. But a gun or a knife weren't the only weapons a man could use to get rid of someone—as that bomb had proved the night before.

A man could use his hands, too. And if someone hurt Elise, Neil might use his to dole out what that person had coming to him: justice.

Her assistant wasn't at her desk; maybe Carmen had already left for the day. It was after five. Neil wasn't sure how he'd stayed away so long, except that he'd been busy with calls to Jordana and Yvette—trying to determine if the police had any leads yet. And when the email had come through, he'd turned that over to Braxville PD as a possible lead—which had led to another interview with his detective sister and her partner.

But he had nothing more to tell them than he'd had the night before. No idea who might want him or Elise dead.

Or was it just him?

Was he the *he* who would get what was coming to him?

If only Elise was what was coming to him...

He wanted her to come to him, to stay with him, to marry him again. But he'd already pushed her too much about that, which he saw the moment she glanced up from her desk and noticed him standing in her doorway. She uttered a weary-sounding sigh and shook her head.

"What?" he asked.

"I'm not leaving with you," she said. "I have too much work to do."

He suspected that wasn't the only reason she didn't want to leave with him, though. "You're going to need a ride home," he said.

She shook her head again. "No. I replaced my car already," she said.

"You hate car shopping."

"Jeremy helped."

"I'm sure he did," Neil said. Was the man trying to replace Elise or him?

With Elise being as beautiful, sexy and damn smart as she was, the deputy mayor probably wanted to be with her—like Neil wanted to be with her. But being with Neil might have been what put her in danger the night before.

The email hadn't said that *she* would get what was coming to her.

"Is that all you're going to say?" she asked, obviously expecting him to say more. Given their history of disagreements, he couldn't blame her.

"No."

She squared her shoulders as if bracing herself for a fight. His stomach muscles, which were already tense with anxiety, tightened more with regret. He didn't mean to argue with her…all the time. Maybe it had just been inbred with him, as a triplet, to fight for what he wanted—the time, the attention, the love.

But love wasn't something a person could take; it had to be given. Freely.

So he swallowed down another proposal before it could escape his lips. And he asked her a different question instead. "Did you get any strange emails today?"

"Emails?" she asked, furrows forming on her forehead. "What kind of emails?"

He'd printed off his—more than one copy, since the police had one that they were going to try to track back to the server from which it had been sent. He pulled the paper from his pocket, unfolded it and slid it across her desk.

The furrows deepened as she read it. "He'll get what's coming to him." She studied it for a moment before raising her head to stare at him. "Who's *he*? You?"

He shrugged. "I don't know. You didn't get one like it?"

She shook her head. "Not unless it went to my junk mail…" She moved her fingers from the note to her keyboard. After striking some keys and moving her mouse, she peered at the computer monitor and shook her head. "I don't see anything like this."

He breathed a sigh of relief. He must have been the target the night before. Not her.

"I'm sorry," he said. "That bomb must have been meant for me."

"I got the phone message yesterday," she pointed out. "I was lured to that warehouse, too."

He flinched with regret. "You must have gotten drawn into my mess for some reason…"

"What reason?" she asked.

He shrugged. "I don't know."

"You don't even know the *he* in that email refers to

you," she pointed out. "It could be about Markus Dexter or your father."

"My father?"

"People are starting to blame him for the illnesses Colton Construction employees are suffering from," she said. "A couple of his former employees even died."

Neil refused to believe that his father could be responsible for those deaths any more than he had been responsible for the dead bodies found within the walls of the warehouse. He shook his head. "If those illnesses have anything to do with Colton Construction, Dex was responsible—not my father."

Elise stared at him for a long moment, her green eyes soft with sympathy or pity. "You really believe that something happened at Colton Construction without your father knowing about it?"

"He didn't know about those bodies in the warehouse," Neil insisted. "There's no way he had anything to do with those murders. So Dex was doing things without my father's knowledge. If there is any contamination at those job sites, it's because of Dex—not my father."

Elise didn't look as convinced of her ex-father-in-law's innocence. But just as she and Neil butted heads, she also butted heads with his father. Like her predecessor, she was opposed to Braxville becoming too urban, too commercial. She'd promised her voters that she would keep it the quaint town it had always been. That was why developers like Neil's father were forced to renovate old buildings instead of building new ones.

"Have you talked to your father about what happened

last night?" she asked. "Hell, have you talked to him about anything that's happened?"

That knot of dread in his stomach tightened even more, and he admitted, "Not yet."

"Don't you think it's time that you do?" she asked. "Especially if he's the one who's put you in danger?"

"He isn't responsible for what happened last night," Neil insisted.

Because his father had always been working while Neil was growing up, he had never been that close to him, but he had no doubt that the man loved his family, loved all his children, and would never consciously put them in harm's way. Neil hoped the same was true of the Colton Construction employees. But if someone blamed Fitz for the men who'd gotten sick and died, maybe they'd figured they would hurt him most by taking away his loved ones.

"I'm not saying he set the bomb," Elise said almost begrudgingly. "But he might know or suspect who did. You need to talk to him."

Even though he knew she was right, Neil groaned with reluctance.

She chuckled then urged, "Talk to him."

Neil owed it to her—if he was the one who'd put her in danger. But just because she hadn't received that email, she wasn't necessarily out of danger now. "I will," he assured her. "As long as you promise me that you'll be careful."

"Of course," she said, and she pressed her hand over her flat stomach as if to shield their unborn child.

Neil wanted to protect them both. In case his father

had any information about what had happened at the warehouse or about who might have sent the email, he had to talk to him. He wasn't sure if he wanted his father to have any answers, though, or if he hoped he was as clueless as Neil was.

He reached for the email printout on Elise's desk, reading those words again. He'll get what's coming to him.

In this context, what the hell did it mean?

Did someone want revenge against Neil? Or against his father?

Before he could pull his hand away from her desk, Elise slid her fingers over his. "You be careful, too," she advised him.

But it was already too late for that warning. Neil was already in too deep—with her. He already wanted too much. And he was undoubtedly going to get his heart broken all over again.

Frustration gnawed at Fitz Colton. He had been in limbo too long, waiting on the health department's report regarding his company. Waiting on his partner being found...

Where the hell had Dex gone?

And what had he done before he left?

He must have murdered those people whose bodies had been found in the warehouse. Had he tried killing Tyler, as well?

And now...

He left his truck parked on the circular drive in front of the house and rushed inside, slamming the door behind himself as he stepped inside. "Lilly!" His voice echoed off the two-story foyer.

She'd worked late yesterday, so she should have been home already. But then she seemed to prefer working to being with him. He felt her slipping away from him just as he felt everything else slipping away— his business, his reputation, his family…

She didn't answer him, but a metallic clang emanated from the vicinity of the kitchen. He found her standing at the sink, staring out the window as she almost absentmindedly scrubbed a pot. The lake, with a light dusting of snow across its partially frozen surface, was beautiful, nearly as beautiful as she was.

But her beauty only intensified his frustration. She wasn't just slipping away from him now. She had slipped away long ago. He'd been gone so much, working so hard to support their family, that he hadn't even noticed until it was too late, until she was too far gone.

"Why didn't you tell me?" he asked.

He hadn't yelled, but she jumped as if he had. "What? Tell you what?" she asked, her voice shaky.

"About Neil, that he was nearly blown up last night," he said. "What did you think I was talking about?"

She shrugged her slender shoulders, then squared them before turning around to face him. "I don't know."

"Why didn't you tell me what happened? I heard he was taken to the hospital last night. Were you there when he was brought in?"

She nodded, and a piece of auburn hair slipped loose from the knot on the back of her head to slide down her cheek. He would have brushed it away for her…years ago. But now, if he tried to touch her, she would push his hand away, push him away. "Yes, I was there," she admitted. "But there are privacy laws—"

"He's my son," he said. "I had a right to know that he was hurt."

"He wasn't hurt," she said. "He's fine."

"What the hell happened?"

"You tell me," she said. "I think you know more than you've told us, Fitz. You're keeping secrets."

"Am I the only one, Lilly?" he asked. But he wasn't sure he wanted to know her secret any more than he wanted everyone to know his. But he knew it was only a matter of time before it all came out.

Hell, he needed to come clean to his family. They deserved the truth.

"I told you that there are privacy laws," she said.

He furrowed his brow and stared at her, failing to comprehend what she was trying to tell him. "I still should have learned about what happened to my boy from my wife, his mother, instead of hearing it in town."

At the coffee shop. He shouldn't keep going to La Dolce Vita, not with how the owner felt about him. Hell, the whole town was starting to feel that way now, but he was too damn proud to hide in shame. Megan Chase, the owner, had taken great delight in telling him about the explosion at the warehouse and, that rumor had it, his son had been inside.

"You were asleep when I came home last night," Lilly said.

He doubted she'd even checked, since he slept in a separate bedroom down the hall from the master suite, which was hers. "You could have woken me up," he suggested. But she hadn't done that in years.

"It's not my place," she murmured.

"You're my wife, his mother. Of course it's your place," Fitz said, frustration nearly consuming him now. What the hell had happened to them?

And was it all his fault?

"It was my place," a deep voice murmured.

Fitz glanced to the doorway, where Neil stood. He wore a suit, like he had come from his office or court. His beard was a little scruffy, though, and his hair a little disheveled, but that was normal for him.

But Fitz had to be sure. "You're okay?"

Neil nodded. But he didn't look certain. He looked unsettled. What did he know?

"We have to talk, Dad," he said.

Fitz had wanted to see his son—to make sure that he was all right. But he didn't want to talk to him...not yet. He wasn't ready to confess all to anyone—least of all someone who might have nearly been killed because of the mistakes that his father had made. Like Dex had gone after Ty, had someone else gone after Neil to get back at *him*?

Chapter 9

If she hadn't planned on working late, Elise would have had the dealer park her new vehicle on the street in front of City Hall. But because she'd known she would surpass the two-hour time limit on the meters, she'd had it delivered to the parking garage down the street, on the other side of the park.

So she had to walk past the park while she was wearing high-heeled boots and a dress. She had the coat on, too, but it wasn't thick enough to ward off the cold. The wind blew through the park, whipping snow flurries around her face and legs. What the hell had she been thinking to dress like this in winter?

Had she dressed up because she'd guessed reporters might be waiting for her? Or because of Neil?

She'd wanted to look good for him. When would

he stop affecting her? When would she stop caring about him?

Never.

She'd accepted that a while ago, that she would always love him, but despite how much she loved him, she couldn't marry him again. Not even for the baby.

At least, not just for the baby.

Which was the only reason he wanted to marry her. To protect the child.

From what?

Had last night really had nothing to do with her? But then why had a message lured her to that warehouse, as well?

She hadn't received the email he had today, though, but maybe it had had nothing to do with what had happened last night.

He'll get what's coming to him.

She shivered, and not just from the cold wind. She'd heard that phrase before, just like Neil must have, during her years as a criminal lawyer in their partnership. Prosecutors said it, police officers, victims.

Was the *he* Neil?

What could he have done that made someone want to kill him, though? Even as hurt, as shattered, as she'd been during their divorce, she had never wished him harm.

No. Whatever was going on, it had nothing to do with Neil personally. It had to be about his family.

Or maybe about her…

That chill rushed over her again, making goose bumps rise on her skin beneath her dress and her coat.

Her heels clicked against the sidewalk as she hastened her step. A sound echoed that click, a heavier, scraping sound as someone followed her. She peered over her shoulder, but she couldn't see much in the faint glow of the twinkling lights wrapped around the street poles. The lamps had been dimmed so that the decorations sparkled more. But now there were too many shadows from the tall trees in the park for Elise to see if someone stood there, watching her.

She was paranoid. Maybe it was just someone else heading to the parking garage for his vehicle. But why had the sound stopped when she turned back?

Why hadn't the person continued walking? There were no shops in this section of street between City Hall and the parking garage, no business into which someone could have gone. Just the park.

So whoever had been behind her was there, lurking in the shadows, not wanting her to see him. Yet…

Not until it was too late?

She reached into the bag slung over her arm, feeling around inside until she found something cold and metallic. She pulled out the small canister of pepper spray. But she should have already had it in her hand; she should have been being careful like she'd promised Neil she would be.

But since she hadn't received the email note that he had, she'd thought she was safe. Maybe that was what the person had intended by not sending her the email. So she would let down her guard. So that she would be alone for the next attack, so that Neil wouldn't be able to save her as he had the last time…

* * *

He could have sent that email to the woman, too. But since she was the mayor now, she probably had a more secure network and other people who screened her correspondence. She might never have seen it, and he'd wanted to be more direct in his threat to her.

He'd already determined that it was good that they'd survived the attempt last night. Dying in the explosion would have been too quick and maybe even a painless way for them to go. They wouldn't have suffered like he'd been suffering for so long.

Going out that way would have been better for them but not for him. No. Now he had time to scare them, to make them rue all the mistakes they'd made.

It was going to be better this way. This way they would learn exactly why they were going to die. And he would be able to make sure that there was no chance of either of them surviving.

Was Elise right…about everything?

Did the attack have everything to do with his father?

Neil should have manned up and had this talk with him long ago. But he hadn't wanted to hear what his father might admit to him. He hadn't wanted to know if the man he'd always idolized had done things for which people might want revenge.

Following his father down the hall to his den, Neil couldn't help but notice how much slower the man moved, how his once-broad shoulders stooped as if carrying a heavy burden. Neil had passed him a little bit in height a while ago, but Fitz seemed even shorter now, as if he were somehow shrinking in size or maybe importance.

With all the problems Colton Construction was facing, Fitz Colton was not the revered and all-powerful man he'd once been in Braxville.

Fitz stepped inside his office, waited for Neil to cross the threshold and then closed the door behind them.

"Mom can't hear this?" Neil asked.

His father shrugged. "I don't know. What do you want to talk about?"

Neil snorted. "Somebody tried to blow me up last night. What do you think I want to talk about?"

"With me?" Fitz asked, his eyes narrowed behind the wire-framed glasses he pushed up his nose. "I didn't even know about it until someone mentioned it in town today."

Neil flinched. "Sorry about that. I thought—"

"Your mother would tell me?" Fitz asked, arching a brown eyebrow, strewn with gray hairs, toward his high forehead. Like his height, his light brown hair had slipped away more and more until he had little left.

"I should have called," Neil said, "but things were crazy after it happened."

He'd found out that he was going to be a father, too. Since his mother hadn't told Fitz about his ER visit last night, she undoubtedly hadn't shared that news, either. He hadn't come here to talk about that, though. Not yet.

Not until he got Elise to accept his proposal. He didn't want his father to think he was shirking his responsibilities again. At least he was pretty sure that was what Fitz had thought when Neil had chosen law school over the family business. His father had never voiced his disapproval, though, but he'd never voiced his approval, either.

"I heard you were with the mayor when the building blew up," Fitz said, his gruff voice emphasizing *mayor* like it was a dirty word.

Neil sighed. "You mean Elise?"

"What were you doing with her?" Fitz asked. "You know she's pretty much shut down my whole company."

"*She* didn't do that. First the police did, and then the health department," Neil reminded him. "But it's your business partner who caused all these problems with your company. Do you know where he is?"

Fitz's face flushed crimson, his eyes widening with shock behind those small lenses. "What the hell do you think? That I'm protecting him?"

"I don't know what to think, Dad," Neil admitted. And he hated having these doubts about his own father. But with all the long hours he'd worked and the events he'd missed because of it, Fitz had proved that Colton Construction meant more to him than his family. There was no way that he could have been completely unaware of everything that had been going on in the company he'd built.

"Wow," Fitz said as he dropped heavily into the chair behind his desk. "Do you actually think I could have had something to do with that explosion last night? That I could have harmed you and Elise?"

Neil shook his head. "No, of course not. But I think your partner might have."

"Why?" Fitz asked.

"The man tried to kill Ty," Neil reminded him.

And his father flinched. "But he thought Tyler was onto him."

"That justifies what he did?" Neil asked, appalled.

Fitz sighed. "No, hell no. But it must have been his motive for shooting at Tyler. What motive would he have for going after you or after Elise?"

"Maybe, like you, he blames the mayor's stand against urban sprawl for everything, for those bodies being discovered."

Fitz glared at him. "The only thing I blame Elise for is not having her own ideas but for blindly carrying on those of her predecessor."

Neil shook his head. "You don't know Elise." She was tough and independent and would never blindly carry on anyone else's ideas. Fitz had never bothered getting to know his former daughter-in-law, though, just as he had never really cared to know his own children.

He hadn't been the one who'd sat with them after school, asking about their days. That had been Mom. She'd always been there for them.

"You didn't give me much of a chance," Fitz said, "before you divorced her."

Neil flinched now. If only he'd given her the time she'd wanted.

But he hadn't wanted them to wind up like his parents, cohabitants in a house but nothing more. How had they had so many children with so little emotion between them? Elise had suggested once that maybe their lack of intimacy was the result of having so many children, that they'd gotten stressed out and drifted apart.

Even divorced, he and Elise were closer than his parents were. But Neil wanted more now. He wanted to be her husband again.

"The divorce was a mistake," he admitted to his dad. An ultimatum he should have known better to ever issue to Elise.

Fitz arched a brow. "Really?"

Neil nodded.

"One you intend to fix?"

"If she'll let me," he said. "But at the moment, we just want to find out who the hell lured us to that warehouse last night to blow us up."

"You were lured?" Fitz asked.

"Yeah, someone left messages claiming the other asked to meet there," Neil shared. "But we didn't."

"So this person is after both of you," Fitz said with surprise. "Not just the mayor?"

"Of course you would think she's the target," Neil murmured.

"Her politics have pissed people off," Fitz said. Furrows formed on his high forehead. "But I doubt that anyone's mad enough to want her dead."

Neil shoved his fingers through his hair, frustrated enough to pull it out. "Then what the hell could this be about?"

"Why are you asking me?" His father's gruff voice had gone even gruffer with his question. "I'm not a detective like your sister. And I certainly had no idea what the hell happened last night, let alone know why."

Neil tilted his head and studied his father's flushed

face. "Really? There's no one who might want revenge against you?"

His face turned redder as he blustered. "For what? What do you think I've done?"

That was his father—always going on the defensive instead of admitting any fault. "Your employees' illnesses—"

"Have nothing to do with you and the mayor," he said. Then added, almost as an afterthought, "Or with me."

"But what if somebody thought you hurt somebody they cared about, and wanted to harm someone you cared about—"

"You're talking nonsense," Fitz interjected. "All of it. What happened to you and the mayor has nothing to do with me or Colton Construction."

Neil wondered if his father truly believed what he was spouting, though. "It happened at a Colton Construction site. The one where those bodies were found. Dex—"

"*Was* my business partner," Fitz said. "So I know one criminal. How many have you and Elise come into contact with in your practice? You certainly know more criminals than I ever will."

He'll get what's coming to him.

Neil had already concluded he'd heard that phrase before, probably many times, during the course of his career in criminal law. But he hadn't always been alone in the practice. Elise had been his partner before she'd become the deputy mayor.

And whoever had left those messages for them the

night before had lured both of them to the warehouse before detonating the bomb.

Someone wanted them both dead. Someone from their shared past…

He cursed.

"What?" Fitz asked.

"You're right," Neil said. "This has to have something to do with the practice."

Which meant that Elise was not safe. In fact, far from it.

He pulled his cell phone from the inside pocket of his jacket.

"Who are you calling?" Fitz asked. "Your sister?"

Jordana might have already figured out what Neil just had. He shook his head. "I need to call Elise." He'd already brought up her contact information, but his call went directly to her voice mail. He cursed again.

He needed to find her. To make sure she was all right. He jerked open the door and rushed out into the hall. His father must have managed to move faster now, because he caught him in the foyer, his hand on Neil's arm holding him back from opening the front door.

"Let the police handle this," Fitz urged him.

"I have to make sure Elise is all right," he said. Because he had that damn feeling again.

That feeling he'd had just minutes before the bomb had exploded. The feeling that compelled him to run… but this time he wasn't going to run away from danger. He would run toward it.

Because he suspected that Elise was in danger.

Chapter 10

Elise held her breath as she stepped inside the dimly lit parking garage. The click of her heels echoed off the concrete floor and walls, louder than her breath would have been had she released it.

She was intent now on listening for the sound of footsteps other than hers. Had that person followed her into the garage?

She clasped the canister of pepper spray more tightly in her hand, which had gotten clammy with sweat despite the cold. She should have been wearing gloves, but she hadn't been thinking of the weather that morning when she'd gotten ready, or she wouldn't have worn the dress and high heels.

Snow swirled even in the garage, through the space between the low walls and low ceilings. Like all new construction, the building was less than two stories high, with plenty of open space. Fortunately, the snow wasn't accumulating enough for her heels to slip, so she hastened her step, nearly trotting as she headed toward the spot where her new vehicle had been parked. She slid her hand, the one not holding the pepper spray, into her pocket and pulled out the key fob. When she clicked it, lights flashed on directly in her face. Blinded, she squinted and looked away, and as she did, a blur of movement caught her attention. Someone jumped out at her.

She spun, the can of pepper spray raised to defend herself. She pressed on the button, but she hadn't taken the safety clip off the top, so nothing came out.

The man held up his hands over his handsome face, though, almost as if he'd been pepper-sprayed before and knew what had nearly happened to him. "It's just me," Jeremy exclaimed. "It's just me."

"What the hell were you doing following me like that?" Elise demanded to know, her heart pounding madly with fear. She wasn't relieved that she knew him, not after the way he'd stalked her down the street.

"I wanted to see your reaction when you saw your new vehicle for the first time," he said, reminding her of a child wanting to surprise his mother with a bouquet of some weeds he'd picked on his way home from school.

Of course, the SUV wasn't a bunch of weeds, though, and Elise had written the check for it. Still, Jeremy had helped her purchase it and had arranged the delivery.

She released a shaky sigh, finally succumbing to relief. Yet she felt compelled to remind him, "I was nearly blown up last night. You didn't consider how that might have made me a little jumpy?"

He gasped and pressed a hand over his heart. "I'm sorry, I wasn't thinking..." He shook his head, but not a single golden strand moved out of place. "But surely what happened last night had to be about Colton or that crazy family of his? It couldn't have had anything to do with you."

She would've liked to think that, too, but she wasn't so sure. Someone had made certain to lure her to join Neil at that warehouse. She shrugged. "I don't know. And because of that, I need to be careful."

And to take the safety cap off the damn can of pepper spray. She wouldn't make that mistake again. She couldn't afford to. She'd been lucky that Jeremy had been the one following her.

Or was she?

He had the most to gain if something happened to her. And he'd been quick to fill her chair before it had even gotten cold this morning. Maybe sending that email to Neil, and the message luring him to the warehouse, had been to make it seem as if he was either the target or the perpetrator.

"That's another reason I followed you," Jeremy said. "To make sure you're safe."

She narrowed her eyes. "But you just said you didn't think I was in danger."

"Not the target," he said. "But because of your association with the Coltons, you could be in danger. Somebody might be trying to get back at them by hurting you, too. I wanted to make sure you got safely to your new car. I would hate for anything to happen to you, Elise."

She nearly snorted in derision. He'd been sucking up like this all day. She hated it.

"I can follow you home, too, and make sure you get safely there," he offered.

She shook her head. "I'll be fine."

"You are going home, right?" he prodded.

Where did he think she was going? To Neil's?

Temptation pulled at her to head in that direction, to head to what had once felt like home to her—the house they'd built together, just as they'd built their law practice.

He'll get what's coming to him.

That phrase in the email sent to Neil sounded so damn familiar. But she'd probably heard it several times while she'd been a criminal lawyer.

Was that what last night had been about? About something that had happened during the years they'd run the practice together? Was that why someone had gone after both of them?

Where she was going wasn't any of her deputy mayor's business, and she was tempted to tell him that. But he had helped her replace her vehicle, so she replied civilly instead. "Yes, I am going home."

"Do you want to stop for dinner somewhere first?" he asked. "You must be hungry."

She should have been; she usually was. But while she hadn't gotten true morning sickness with her pregnancy, she felt slightly nauseated all day instead, just enough to curb her appetite.

Maybe that was less a physical side effect of her pregnancy and more an emotional one. She was tough and independent, but she'd never wanted to be a single mother like her mom. She wasn't going to accept Neil's proposal, either, not when the baby was the only reason he was proposing. "I'm too tired to be hungry," she admitted. "I didn't get much sleep last night."

"Of course—because of the explosion."

The explosion hadn't been the reason; Neil had. When was she going to be able to resist her attraction to him? Maybe when she was too big to see her feet.

"Yes," she replied. "So I'm going straight to bed." Alone. Not that Jeremy was inviting himself to join her. Despite how solicitous he was with her, he had never crossed the line into open flirting. She had no idea if he had a crush on her, or if he was just sucking up to the boss.

The person she didn't want in her bed tonight was Neil—because she wanted him more than she wanted sleep. But she needed to get some rest—for herself and for the baby that was developing inside her.

"Thank you, Jeremy, for helping me get this vehicle," she said. "I'll see you in the morning."

Before he could say anything else, she quickly climbed into the new SUV and closed the door behind herself. She drew in a deep breath of relief while also inhaling the scent of new leather. Maybe car shopping wasn't so bad after all.

If she hadn't been so tired, she might have taken the new vehicle for a spin around town to take in all the Christmas decorations. But she drove directly to her condo. As she headed down the street toward her unit, she automatically lifted her hand toward her visor. The garage door opener was in her other vehicle, though, and had undoubtedly burnt up with it. But between the dealer, Jeremy and her condo association, the new SUV had been programmed with the information from the opener so that the garage door began to lift as she approached.

She smiled with appreciation—until she noticed that the service door between the garage and the house stood open. She hadn't left it that way.

Someone else must have left it open. When they'd gone inside or when they'd left?

She stopped the SUV on the condo's short driveway while she pondered what to do. Chances were that the person had already left, though. And she had the pepper spray and knew to remove the safety cap now. So she turned off the SUV and stepped out onto the driveway. The smart thing to do was call the police, though. So she pulled out her cell instead of the pepper spray and hit the emergency call button.

While waiting for the operator to pick up, she moved closer to the condo, listening for any sounds from inside. But she hadn't noticed the sounds right around her—of someone approaching.

Strong arms suddenly closed around her as someone grabbed her. A scream burned the back of her throat, but before she could release it, a hand covered her mouth.

And just then the operator picked up, her voice emanating from the cell phone. "What's your emergency?"

* * *

"Why the hell are we responding to a B&E?" Reese grumbled from the passenger seat as Jordana turned on the lights and sirens.

She only spared him a glance, her total focus on the road. She had to get there before anything happened, like another bomb being set to explode.

"You should have recognized the address," Jordana admonished him. "It's the mayor's."

Reese cursed. "You think someone's trying to make another attempt on her life?"

"I don't believe it's a coincidence that her condo's getting broken into a day after the explosion. Do you?" she asked, well aware of her partner's cynicism.

There was no way Reese Carpenter believed in coincidences or fate or maybe anything at all. She had once been like that herself until she'd met Clint and fallen so deeply in love.

Reese cursed again. "No, it's not a coincidence."

"So she must have been the target," Jordana mused, and some of the tightness in her chest eased somewhat. Hopefully, Neil was not in any real danger, then.

And maybe this was all about the mayor. Not him…

She'd nearly lost one of her brothers the month before, when Ty was shot. She did not want to lose Neil. But if he knew that his ex-wife was in danger…

Jordana doubted she would be able to keep him away from the mayor's condo, especially if Elise was anywhere near it. The dispatcher hadn't known who'd called to report the break-in. It could have been Elise. Hell, it could have been Neil who'd called, or who had broken into the place.

Even after divorcing Elise, he never seemed to stay away from her. But if she was the one in danger, he might get killed, too, if he got too close to his ex.

Neil breathed a sigh of relief that stirred Elise's hair. He was so damn glad that she was all right. But then he turned her in his arms. "What were you thinking?"

"What the hell were you thinking to grab me like that?" she asked.

"I was stopping you from going inside," he said, "when I noticed that the door was open between the garage and your utility room."

"I noticed that, too, so I damn well was not going inside," she assured him.

"Good. Get in your SUV and drive away from here," he instructed her. But knowing that she rarely listened to him, he guided her toward her new vehicle and the driver's door she'd left open.

"You want me to leave?" she asked.

He nodded. "At least until the police arrive and secure your place."

"Okay…" But she stopped before climbing behind the steering wheel and turned back to him. "What are you going to do?"

"I'm going inside," he replied.

Elise's hands went to his chest, but instead of embracing him, she pushed him back. "What the hell are you thinking?"

"I'm thinking I might be able to catch the damn person before he gets away." Unless he spent too much time out here arguing with her. But when he turned toward the garage, Elise grabbed his arm.

"You can't go in there."

"I can't let him get away," Neil said as he pulled free of her. "Get in your SUV and lock the door!"

"Neil!"

"I'm sure he's already gone," Neil assured her. But as he got closer to that open door, noises emanated from within the condo. A heavy thud as something struck the wood floor.

Careful to be quiet, he eased through the opening and stepped inside the back hall. The doors to the closet on one side of it stood open, as if someone had been looking for something. Coats had been knocked from their hangers. He turned the other way and walked down the hall to the kitchen, where he found cupboard doors and drawers open.

Someone had ransacked the place. And must still be ransacking it...

Another thud echoed from just beyond the kitchen.

He moved toward the noise, but as he did, a shadow rushed toward him, shoving him so hard down the hall that he was knocked all the way back into the open closet. Losing his balance, he fell into the pile of coats.

The shadow passed by him, out the open door, to where he'd left Elise alone on the driveway.

What the hell had he been thinking?

He shouted her name in warning. But it was too late. The person had to have reached her already and maybe hurt her or worse.

Chapter 11

He came barreling toward her, such intensity on his face that Elise had no idea what he might do to her. She knew what she wanted to do: launch herself at him and lash out at him for what he'd put her through.

Fury gripped Elise so fiercely that she trembled with it, her body shaking. "You could have been killed," she admonished Neil.

"I'm fine," he said. "What about you?" His hands shook a little as he reached for her, helping her out of the SUV.

When he'd gone inside the house, she'd thought about following him, about trying to protect him. But he wasn't the only one she needed to worry about protecting.

She pressed a hand over her stomach. Fearing for

the baby as well as for Neil, she'd hopped into her new vehicle and clicked the locks. Guilt had gripped her, though. Guilt that she wasn't backing up Neil inside the condo, but she'd known the police were due to arrive soon. Sirens had been wailing in the distance, just loud enough that if the intruder was inside the condo yet, he would have heard them.

She wasn't sure if the intruder had heard them or if he'd heard Neil instead. But he'd erupted from the house just seconds ago. Luckily, he'd run past the SUV without noticing her. He'd probably been in a hurry to escape the police cars that arrived, with flashing lights and ear-splitting sirens, just seconds after his departure.

She flinched over the noise and the glare of the lights but nodded. "I'm fine."

Her heart and pulse raced yet with the fear she'd felt for Neil's safety. She'd been so scared for him, and when the other man had run out first, she'd worried that the police were going to be too late. That something had already happened to Neil—something horrible.

Fortunately Neil had been just seconds behind the intruder, moving with such speed that he seemed to be unharmed. She had thrown open the door of her SUV to stop him from pursuing the guy, though.

"Did you recognize him?" Neil asked. "Do you know who he is?"

She shook her head. "No. Did you?"

"I didn't get a look at his face," Neil said, his voice gruff with disappointment.

"Me, neither."

The man, tall and muscular, had been wearing a

hoodie pulled tight around his face. All she'd seen was the side of that hood, not any of his profile, as he'd rushed past her. But he was big, bigger than Neil.

When Neil had helped her out of the SUV, her entire body was shaking with fear, and she'd grabbed his arms to steady herself. Now she clutched his forearms, which tensed beneath his jacket. She was tempted to pull Neil even closer. To hold him tight with relief that he was all right.

But she was still so damn mad that he'd put himself in danger. She was not the only one, as Detective Colton ran up to join them.

"What the hell are you two doing here?" Jordana demanded to know.

"I live here," Elise reminded her ex-sister-in-law. "I don't know why your brother is here." She hadn't had time to ask him why he'd showed up when he had. She'd been too worried about that open door. "And I sure don't know why the hell he's trying to play superhero."

The only thing she knew for certain was that if he kept it up, he was unlikely to live to see their child born. If whoever was after them didn't kill him, she probably would, for risking his damn life.

When Jordana whirled toward him, Neil held up his hands to ward her off like he should have warded off the intruder. But there hadn't been time…

No time for him to catch the guy or catch himself from tumbling into the closet. Despite the cold night breeze blowing around the driveway, heat coursed through Neil—the heat of anger and frustration.

If only he'd been faster. If only he could have stopped the man. Then this would all be over; they would be safe.

He wasn't safe now, not from the angry women glaring at him.

"You're a lawyer," Jordana said, as if he had to be reminded. "Not a police officer. Once you two realized the place had been broken into, you should have left until the police could get here to secure the scene."

"Instead he went inside," Elise informed his sister. "He tried to catch him."

Jordana gasped and whirled toward him. "That was so damn stupid, Neil. And dangerous."

He shrugged off her concern. "I'm fine." Only his ego—and maybe his ass—had gotten bruised. Which made him wonder.

"I'm not even sure it was the person who set up the bomb," he said. "It could have just been a burglar."

"We'll have Elise check to see what's missing," Jordana said. But when Elise started toward the open door to her condo, she caught her arm. "After we clear the place."

"Clear the place?" Elise asked, her voice cracking with fear. "You think there could have been a couple of them inside the condo?" She reached out and smacked Neil's shoulder. "And you went in there unarmed and outnumbered! You could have been killed."

"I'm fine," he repeated.

But why hadn't the intruder taken the opportunity to kill Neil when he'd had the chance? Or Elise, as well? She'd just been sitting in the SUV in the driveway. The man had probably heard the sirens, though, and had worried that he was about to get caught if he didn't leave in a hurry. And he had left in a real hurry.

"Even if there was just one guy, he could have had a gun," Elise said. "You're lucky you didn't get shot."

"Or worse," Jordana added. "He could have been setting another bomb in there. That's why you two need to clear out of here."

Neil sucked in a breath of shock. He'd been so intent on catching the guy that he hadn't realized what the man actually might have been doing inside Elise's condo.

Setting another explosive device.

That was why he hadn't bothered to stop and kill Neil. It was why he'd been in such a damn hurry to get the hell out of there, too.

Even now he could be out there, somewhere beyond the police cars, waiting to detonate it.

Jordana must have considered the same thing because she waved toward Elise's SUV. "Unless you want to lose this one, too, I suggest you get in and get the hell out of here until the bomb squad clears your place."

Elise gasped and nodded. For once she was speechless.

So was Neil.

He hadn't considered that just being in the proximity could have put her in danger, too. He should have made her leave the area, and he never should have gone inside alone.

"I'm sorry," he murmured, to both women.

Sorry that he hadn't been thinking.

He had just been so intent on ending this so that

they were no longer in danger. But they weren't just in danger. They were waiting for this person to strike out at them again and not knowing when it might happen.

Was it now?

Damn it!

Once he'd broken inside her condo through the side door of the garage, he had allowed himself to get distracted with thoughts of how unfair it all was. How she had so much while some other people had so little.

Not even life.

And he'd let his rage over the injustice of it all consume him.

Instead of putting his plan into motion, he'd smashed her stuff, taking his anger out on inanimate objects instead of the people who deserved it.

Who'd earned it.

And their reward for what they'd done was going to be death.

He stared through the windshield of the vehicle he'd stolen in another city, from a retirement center so that the owner might not even realize it was gone for a while. He'd parked it on the street outside the complex, and he sat inside it, in the dark, watching. Waiting.

Lights flashed as more official vehicles rolled into the complex. He chuckled as he saw the special response vehicles. What the hell did they think he'd done?

There hadn't been time for that.

No. His plan tonight had been to just send them a message. And maybe he had.

But now he wanted more. He wanted this over. *Them* over...

He couldn't get to them here, though, not with all the police officers swarming around. So he would wait until they left.

And he would follow.

The next time he came this close to his prey, he would take them out for good.

Chapter 12

Worried about the danger to her neighbors, Elise had refused to leave the condo complex. She'd gone only as far as the entrance, where everyone stood after being evacuated.

"I'm sorry," she murmured to her neighbors, like Neil had murmured to her and his sister earlier.

She hadn't accepted his apology. She was still too angry with him. But most of her neighbors accepted hers. "Not your fault, Mayor," one of the older men assured her. "Can't help that some crazy is going after you." He cast a suspicious glance Neil's way.

He was some crazy—or at least he'd acted crazy when he'd charged into the condo unarmed and unprepared. She sighed and shook her head, amazed and grateful that he had not been injured. She was still angry that he'd taken such a chance with his life.

She slid her hand over her belly, thinking of the life growing inside her—the one that Neil had helped create. He'd wanted so badly to become a father, and he could have missed the opportunity entirely if something had happened to him.

Still could miss it if he kept taking foolish chances like that...

She'd been tempted, too, though. She wanted this over, and the real crazy person who was determined to kill them caught, as much as Neil wanted him caught. But before she'd let herself walk inside the condo, she'd reminded herself that she wasn't putting just herself in danger. She was endangering the baby, too.

"Bomb squad is leaving," Neil remarked beneath his breath, as he pointed toward the black panel van passing the entrance to turn onto the street.

Elise expelled a shaky breath of relief. There must not have been a bomb, then. She hadn't put her neighbors in danger. This time.

Until this person was caught, however, she could unwittingly cause them harm.

"You can all return to your homes," Detective Carpenter told the crowd gathered around the entrance. "Everything is fine. We've thoroughly searched the entire area and determined there is no threat."

The intruder was gone, and he'd left nothing dangerous behind him. Elise couldn't summon any relief, though. She knew he'd be back.

"We can leave now," Neil said. "We know your neighbors are okay."

Maybe he knew her better than she thought he did—since he knew her neighbors' safety had been her primary concern. "I'm not leaving," she said.

"You can't stay," Neil argued. "If you do, he'll come back."

She doubted that he would return tonight—with all the police officers on the scene. But he would come back…sometime.

"You can't leave," Detective Carpenter interrupted them. "Not until you give your statements."

"I already spoke to my sister," Neil said.

Reese shook his head. "I don't think she heard much of what you told her. She was too damn mad. In fact, she hasn't cooled off a whole hell of a lot yet." He sent Neil a pitying glance. "Maybe you should leave."

"I'm staying," Elise said. The thought of someone inside her home, touching her things…

She shivered.

"Then let's get you inside, Mayor," Detective Carpenter said. "It's freezing out here."

She'd been so angry she hadn't noticed the cold. But she gratefully followed him back to her condo.

Neil, of course, was right behind her. But when she started across her threshold, he caught her arm. "You may not want to see this," he warned her.

"What happened?" she asked. "I thought there was no bomb."

"Still looks like one went off inside," Reese remarked. "The guy was sure angry about something."

"I can relate," Elise murmured as she stepped inside her condo. From the mess, it looked more like a tornado had swept through her home than an intruder. Everything had been upended, with pictures torn from the walls, drawers emptied onto the floor.

She gasped as she noticed the contents of one of those drawers. Broken glass surrounded the cracked frame of her and Neil's wedding portrait.

Instead of being upset, as she was, Neil grinned when he saw it. He picked it up from the floor and stared at their smiling faces. "You kept it…"

"In a drawer," she pointed out. "I'd pretty much forgotten it was there."

Except for all the times she pulled it out and stared at it, at how happy they'd been that day…and wondered what had happened, how it had all gone so wrong.

That was why she couldn't accept his proposal—not when she knew how devastated she would be if they failed again. They'd started out last time with so much love and hope and promise.

Jordana had noticed the shattered wedding portrait when the bomb squad had first cleared her to enter the condo. She couldn't understand why her brother would grin at the broken picture.

She and Clint weren't even married yet, but she could already imagine that she would be as shattered as that portrait if they ever divorced. But they would never do that. They loved each other too much.

She'd once thought that Neil and Elise had loved each other, too. The way they were looking at each other now, though, wasn't too different than how they'd looked at each other in that portrait. Maybe the love was still there. But there was also pain and disillusionment, which reminded her of her parents.

She cleared her throat, drawing their attention to her. "Have you had a chance to look through the condo and determine if anything's missing?" she asked Elise.

Elise shook her head.

"It's late," Neil said. "She doesn't have time to do an inventory. I'm going to take her home with me."

"I'm not a stray dog," Elise said, her voice sharp with indignation.

"It would take you all night to do an inventory of this mess," Neil pointed out. "And you need your sleep, especially now."

If not for the dark circles beneath Elise's pretty green eyes, Jordana would have asked why he'd said that, but the mayor looked so tired it was easy to understand why she needed sleep. She probably hadn't gotten much rest after the explosion the night before.

And now this.

"Did either of you get a good look at the intruder?" Jordana asked. She hadn't had time to question them earlier—given how angry she'd been with them for putting themselves in danger and with the potential hazard of another bomb being planted in the condo.

Elise described a big man with a hood pulled tight covering most of his head and face, and Neil nodded in agreement but added nothing more.

Jordana sighed with frustration. It was pretty damn hard to put out an APB for someone matching that description. If she did, almost half of Braxville would be pulled in for questioning.

"You have no idea who might be coming after the two of you?" she asked.

They both tensed, as if they were holding something back. Or had come to some kind of realization they were hesitant to admit.

"What?" she asked when neither answered her. "Who?"

Elise gave her an almost pitying glance. "Maybe it has something to do with your father—"

"We're already looking at Markus Dexter for it," Reese interjected.

"I meant someone else—someone who might have gotten sick or worse while working for your father."

"We don't know that Colton Construction is really responsible for anybody getting sick," Neil said, coming to their father's defense. But then that was what he did—he defended criminals.

Jordana didn't want to believe that their father could be one, though. It wasn't possible. But what if someone else believed that? "Why go after you two, though, to get back at Dad? Why not all of us?"

"Maybe we're just the first two," Elise suggested.

Neil shook his head. "It doesn't make sense. If somebody really wanted to hurt my dad, why hurt you?"

Elise flinched. "True. Something happening to me would make him happy."

Neil shook his head again. "No."

"I did have another thought," Elise admitted.

And Neil finished that thought for her as if he'd read

her mind, "That it could be someone from when we were in practice together?"

Elise nodded.

"Of course," Reese said, "you guys represented criminals, so maybe one of them didn't like the deal you got him."

He'll get what's coming to him.

That was the email Neil had received earlier that day. "Or maybe someone thinks you got a criminal too good a deal."

"But why wait until now to come after us?" Elise asked. "We've not been partners for a few years now."

In business or in their personal lives.

Jordana shrugged. "I don't know. But *we'll* look into it. Not you two. We're the detectives. You need to stay out of this."

Neil held up his hands. "I just want to take Elise home."

"This is my home," Elise said, but as she looked around the ransacked condo, her shoulders slumped with defeat.

"My home," Neil said. "I have the top-of-the-line security system. You have just that doorbell camera."

Which hadn't helped when the intruder had come through the garage.

"Just to be sure that your system is really top-notch, we'll check out the house before you go there," Jordana recommended. "We'll make sure it's clear for you."

Neil must have been tired, too, because he didn't fight her on this, either, while the lawyer in him usually argued so much that it seemed like he had come out of their mother's womb arguing. That was why she didn't tell him about the other thing she'd done. She didn't want him protesting or claiming that she was getting overprotective. After what had happened tonight—what could have happened—she wasn't being protective enough.

Neil was so damn stubborn and independent that he would get himself killed if he wasn't careful. Tonight he'd proved he wasn't being wary enough, so Jordana would be cautious for him.

Neil's eyes narrowed as he studied her face. Clearly he suspected that she was up to something. But once again he didn't argue. Maybe he'd realized that she was only concerned about his safety.

He turned his attention to Elise then, urging her to pack up a suitcase so they could leave. And the look on his face…

It was so like his lovesick expression in that wedding portrait that Jordana wasn't just worried about his physical safety now. She was concerned he might get his heart broken all over again.

Neil followed Elise's new SUV away from the condo toward his place. But he was tense with apprehension that she might suddenly turn off and head to a hotel instead of his house. The fact that she'd agreed to come home with him either meant that she was scared or just too exhausted to protest.

Either reason had his heart aching with regret. He'd fallen for Elise because of her fierce independence, because of her conviction to her opinions. Unfortunately, those were also the things that infuriated him the most about her. But he still didn't want her to lose them—to lose herself—like she'd once admitted she feared would happen when she moved to his hometown and became a Colton.

But Neil didn't want to lose her, either. That could have happened tonight if she had gone inside her condo before he got there, or if the intruder had harmed her when he ran out of her place. Or another explosive had been put in the condo.

His stomach lurched with dread over the danger she was in, over the danger they were both in.

Had a bomb been planted at his house?

Braxville PD vehicles filled the driveway. They were checking it out, as Jordana had insisted. He didn't mind his big sister's protectiveness, not in this case, not when she was also protecting her unborn niece or nephew, albeit unknowingly, as well as him and Elise.

Elise parked alongside the curb outside the home she had once willingly left just as she'd left him. Of course, he'd asked for the divorce, but he would have taken it all back…if she'd opposed it. But she, who fought over everything, hadn't fought for them.

She stepped out of the SUV and pulled open the passenger door of his to say, "Where are we going to go until they clear the house?"

"Have you eaten?" he asked.

She shook her head.

"Elise, you need to eat." She should be eating for two now, resting for two. Everything she did affected their baby as well as herself.

The fear, the danger, the exhaustion.

She grimaced.

And his heart thudded with alarm. "What's wrong? Are you all right?"

She sighed. "You know how much I usually love food, but I've been queasy the past few weeks."

"Morning sickness?"

"All-day-long sickness," she said. Her stomach grumbled, and her grimace turned to a smile. "But I should probably eat something."

"Me, too," he said. He'd been so consumed with finding out who was after them that he probably hadn't eaten, either. He couldn't remember grabbing much more than a snack earlier. As he turned off his street to head back toward town, he noticed headlight beams in his rearview as another vehicle followed them.

Jordana was checking out his house, but what about everywhere else? She couldn't keep them safe—not from someone following them.

It was up to Neil now. He had to keep his family from harm.

Chapter 13

For someone who kept proposing to her, Neil sure wasn't paying Elise much attention. Instead of talking to her, he stared silently out the restaurant window. Hungrier than she'd realized, she had been preoccupied with shoveling the diner special of meatloaf and mashed potatoes into her face, so she hadn't noticed his silence until now.

He hadn't even touched his plate, which tempted her to reach across to steal his burger. Instead, she settled for just a fry. Then another...

As she swiped one through the ketchup he'd squirted onto the plate, she remarked, "What's got your attention outside?"

He glanced at her then—just briefly—before gazing back out the window.

She turned to peer out, as well, but saw only her own reflection and his in the darkened glass. "What is it?" she asked.

Was someone out there?

"Uh, just all the decorations," he said. "They're really pretty this year."

"They're the exact same ones we had last year." Twinkle lights and lit-up wreaths wrapped around every light pole. But they were pretty.

She glanced at Neil's phone that he'd left sitting on the tabletop next to his formerly untouched plate. She grabbed another fry and remarked, "Since your sister hasn't called with the all clear, we should get a tree before we head back, and decorate it."

Neil whirled away from the window and toward her now, his blue eyes wide with surprise and delight. "You want to get a tree with me?"

She chuckled. "Well, it might be a good trial run. Make sure we can keep that alive before we have a kid." She trailed off as her joke fell flat to her own ears. With someone trying to kill them, keeping their child and each other alive wasn't going to be easy. "Who do you think it is?" she asked. "Who's after us?"

He shook his head. "I don't know."

"Maybe we should skip the tree and head back to your office and go through our old case files," she suggested.

"Jordana said to leave the investigation to her," he reminded her, and his attention returned to the window.

She narrowed her eyes and studied his face. "And since when do you leave anything to anyone else?"

"You should talk," he shot back at her.

She chuckled. "I know. That's one of the too many things we have in common that make us incompatible."

He flinched. "We are not incompatible."

"If we weren't, we would still be married," she pointed out.

A twinkle brightened his blue eyes, and he said, "We could be if you would say yes."

Her heart leaped—at that twinkle—and at the temptation to say yes. But she couldn't summon the trust to make the leap—not in herself and her judgment, and not in him. Not after he had ended their marriage so easily.

She shook her head. "Don't…" Her appetite gone, or at least finally sated, she pushed her empty plate away. "I'm tired. I think I should just check into a hotel."

"No, Elise," he said as he shoved his plate aside, too. "I won't pressure you anymore."

"It's not just that," she said. "I really am tired, and it's taking them too long to clear the house." Which meant that they'd probably found something they'd had to clear. Another explosive?

He glanced at his phone. "She texted a while ago. It's clear. We can go home."

She shook her head now. "No, you can never go home again."

She had to remind herself of that more than him. The house they'd built together wasn't her home. Not anymore.

And it never would be again…

* * *

Neil wanted to take Elise home more than anything. But he didn't want to take along whoever was following them. And he was certain that someone was.

He hadn't been staring out that window at decorations. He'd been watching the car parked a little way down the street, and the dark shadow behind the wheel, to see if the person would step out. Why just sit there?

Unless he'd been staring at Neil and Elise through that restaurant window, waiting for them to leave.

Neil probably should have texted Jordana back and let her know that someone could be following them. But what if he was wrong? Then he would be upsetting Elise for no reason. And in her current condition, he didn't want to keep upsetting her, especially after what had happened earlier at her condo. She'd been furious with him and devastated over the damage to her things. All this fear, stress and anxiety could not be good for their baby.

"Let's get that tree," he suggested as they stepped out of the diner.

She tilted her head up toward him, tempting him to lower his head, to brush his mouth across hers. He wanted to kiss her so badly. But she narrowed her eyes and studied his face. "What's up with you?"

"It was your idea," he reminded her. He also wanted to walk a little closer to that vehicle, to see if the person was still sitting behind the wheel. The Christmas tree stand was in a small parking lot just a couple of storefronts from the diner. When Elise started toward it, his stomach tightened. He didn't want her any closer to whoever might have followed them, but he also didn't want her out of his sight, out of his reach. He caught her hand in his.

Startled to find her skin so cold, he remarked, "You're not wearing gloves."

"You're not, either," she pointed out.

They'd both been so preoccupied that morning that he understood how the gloves had been forgotten. He was still preoccupied with her safety. One of her boots slipped on the sidewalk, and she stumbled into him. He caught her, holding her upright. He'd been concerned about the man in the parked car; now he was worried about her. He glanced toward that vehicle and noticed the shadow was gone. Nobody sat behind the steering wheel of what was actually a station wagon–type SUV.

Where the hell had the driver gone?

Neil swiveled his neck, looking behind them—in front of them—and to the side. He hadn't noticed anyone getting out of the vehicle.

"You lost him?" Elise asked, her voice pitched to a low whisper.

"Who?" Neil asked, feigning confusion.

"Whoever you were watching from the diner window."

Of course she'd noticed. Elise rarely missed anything, except how much he loved her. But he wondered if she had ever really trusted his love or him. And thanks to the stubbornness that was so much a part of both of them, she probably never would.

"I thought someone might have been following us," he murmured. "I could just be paranoid."

"Probably," she agreed. "But call Jordana anyway."

"For paranoia?"

"You don't believe it's just that," she said.

He sighed and shrugged. "I don't know what to believe." But he wanted to find out. Where could the person have gone from that vehicle?

He peered around him, looking more for hiding places than at the trees on the Christmas tree lot. Elise's attention left him for a moment as she walked around a few of the cut trees. She stopped near a giant fir tree, gestured at it and murmured, "That would look beautiful in the great room."

He loved the look on her face, the awe. It was the same as it had been the first time they'd gone Christmas tree shopping. She and her mother had never had a real tree. The apartments where they'd lived hadn't allowed them nor had the space for one like this. They'd only had room for a small artificial tree. So when they'd designed the house, Neil had made certain that there was room for the biggest tree he could fit inside the house. For her...

And for the little girl she'd once been, the one who'd longed for more than her single mother had been able to provide.

"That's an awesome tree," he agreed. "But it's not going to fit on the roof of my SUV."

"We deliver," the attendant said.

Neil paid the man before giving him his address for delivery tomorrow. But he pitched his voice low as he did, not wanting anyone to overhear the details. But if that vehicle had followed him from his street, then the driver already knew where he lived.

The house was clear and safe, though. Jordana had assured him of that. He needed to bring Elise home.

But that sensation…that creepy sensation of being watched…

It had the skin crawling on his back as a chill raced down his spine. Whoever it was must have been behind them, staring holes into him. That was where the driver had gone; he'd gotten out to follow them on foot.

Neil led Elise quickly across the street to his SUV, keeping his arm around her until he opened the passenger's door for her. Then he helped her onto the seat.

She caught his arm before he could pull away and close the door. "What are you going to do?"

While she didn't know how much he loved her, maybe she knew him a little better than he'd thought she did. A smile tugged at his lips. "What makes you think I'm going to do anything?"

"Because I know how damn stubborn you are," she said.

"I'm just going to walk around a little bit, see where the driver of that car I was watching might have gone."

She shook her head, tousling her golden-blond hair around her shoulders. One tendril brushed against his cheek. Her hair was so soft, so silky. He wanted to lose his fingers in it while he kissed her lips. "It's too dangerous," she protested.

"Not if it's just someone shopping in one of the stores around here," he pointed out.

"Do you know what the person looks like?"

"I'll know when they return to their vehicle."

"Watch it from here," she said.

He shook his head. "I can't see it."

But the driver could see them if he was inside the vehicle; he could see when they pulled out and then follow them. But if the person intended to follow them, then he had to return to his vehicle. Now. Before Neil drove off.

"It'll just take a second," Neil assured her. "And I'll be right back."

"Neil!"

He covered her mouth with his, kissing her quickly but hotly before pulling back to close her door. He clicked the fob to lock the SUV, but that didn't mean she couldn't unlock and step out of it.

He only hoped she waited long enough that he had time to draw the attention of whoever was following them and lead him away from her.

He had to end this. He had to end *them*. Soon.

When they'd left the condo in separate vehicles, he hadn't known which one to follow, but at least they'd headed the same direction, to the same place. The lawyer's house. But there had been police vehicles parked there, too. Thinking they'd had too much protection, he'd almost left. But just before he'd pulled away, he'd noticed the mayor get into the lawyer's vehicle. And they'd driven off again—with him following.

This was going to be his best chance to take them both out. But he had to be patient. He couldn't act rashly or let his rage control him, as he had earlier, at the mayor's condo.

What he'd done to her place—to her things—had to have sent her the message, though. That she didn't deserve the things she had, the life she was living…

Not after the mistake she'd made. It was past time she paid for it, for the justice she'd cost him. He'd had to wait so damn long.

And now he was able to act, to release all that rage.

His fury had earlier gotten out of hand, at her condo.

He could have been caught. And that wouldn't do. He was doling out justice; he wasn't going to have it dealt to him.

Chapter 14

He could not have gone far, not if he was following them.

Not even if he was just someone from Neil's neighborhood who had decided to head downtown at the same damn time they had.

He wouldn't have parked far from whatever business he intended to patronize, especially if he was like Elise, who had an aversion to walking too far or too fast. So the driver of the car, which Neil was pretty damn certain had followed them, had to be close.

Close to him and close to Elise. Neil shivered at the thought. She hadn't put herself in danger back at the condo, though—not like he had. So she would stay in the locked vehicle.

At least that was what he was counting on.

He hadn't counted on it taking so long for whoever belonged to that vehicle to come back, though. But maybe the person had noticed him loitering near it and knew that Neil was waiting for him to return.

A shadow fell across the sidewalk a short distance away, where a narrow alley separated a couple of shops. If he ducked in there, the person wouldn't see that Neil was still watching his vehicle. He glanced around, making certain no one appeared to be looking at him, before he eased backward into that space between the buildings. He wasn't sure it was actually an alley, though; it didn't seem wide enough for even a small car to traverse. It was also so dimly lit that he didn't notice anyone else standing in the shadows.

Until strong arms wrapped around him, pulling him farther from the street. He'd walked right into the trap of whoever was following him.

"Son of a bitch!" he yelled as he began to struggle.

He had to fight—for himself, for Elise and for their unborn baby. And it was a fight he couldn't lose—for all their sakes.

Ty grunted with pain as Neil's elbow struck close to his healing wound. "Damn it! Stop! And you better watch what you call me—since we share the same mother."

Neil jerked free of his hold and whirled around on him. "What the hell are you doing grabbing me in a dark alley?"

"What the hell are you doing walking into dark alleys when someone's trying to kill you?"

"I didn't realize it might be you," Neil sarcastically replied.

"If it was me trying to kill you, you would already be dead," Ty warned him. "Jordana was right to call me. You need protection all right—protection from yourself."

Neil cursed. "I don't need my older siblings acting like I'm a stupid little kid anymore."

"Then don't be stupid," Ty replied.

Neil cursed again.

Ty chuckled, but he wasn't amused. From what Jordana had told him about the explosion, their brother was in serious danger. "Do you really want to be Dex's next victim?"

Like Ty very nearly had been, when the son of a bitch had shot him. A twinge of pain passed through his old wound again. He was healing, but not as quickly as he wanted. He had to be a hundred percent, especially now…because he wanted to keep his brother safe.

"I don't think I'm in any danger of that," Neil replied.

Ty snorted. "You just nearly got blown up and you don't think you're in any danger? You must have hit your head—hard—in the blast!"

"I don't think I'm in any danger from Dex," Neil said. "He has no reason to come after me and Elise."

"He didn't really have a reason to come after me, either," Ty said. "He just thought he did. Maybe, for some reason, he thinks he has a reason to take out the two of you, too."

Neil shook his head. "No, Elise and I are both pretty

certain this is related to one of our cases when we were in partners in the law firm."

Ty groaned.

"What?"

"You guys handled a lot of cases…" Which meant a lot of potential suspects.

"Yes, we did," Neil said.

"So it might take a while to figure out who the hell is coming after you," he said.

"Jordana tells me to stay out of it, but she has you helping her?" Neil asked, his voice gruff with indignation.

Ty could have teased him about his resentment, because teasing was one of an older brother's responsibilities, but taking care of his younger siblings was also one of them. "Jordana has a partner. She hasn't asked me to play detective like you're trying to do. She asked me to watch out for you and make sure the person trying to kill you doesn't succeed before she has a chance to figure out who it is."

All wounded pride, Neil tensed. Maybe that was part of a younger brother's role—to get all defensive. "I can take care of myself. I can also figure out who's trying to kill me and Elise."

Ty snorted in derision. "That's why it was so damn easy for me to grab you."

"Seriously, if I hadn't noticed you following me, I wouldn't have stepped into this alley to wait for you to go back to your car," Neil said. "So it's your fault for blowing your security detail."

"I didn't blow it," Ty said.

"Then how did I see you?" Neil challenged him. "Jordana shouldn't have called you. You must be still recuperating from your gunshot wound."

"I'm fine. Fully recovered," Ty said, and it wasn't a complete lie. He was pretty much recovered. "And you didn't see me. I'm driving a truck. Not a car."

Neil shook his head. "It might be a small SUV, but I wouldn't call it a truck."

"No, it's a truck," Ty maintained, his brow furrowing as he pondered his brother's confusion. "Are you that unaware of vehicle makes and models?" Wouldn't a lawyer have to have some knowledge of them to defend alleged hit-and-run and under-the-influence drivers?

"I know the difference between a truck and a car," Neil assured him. "Some people call their SUVs trucks."

"Not me," Ty said. "What the hell did you see following you?"

"A station wagon–type vehicle. Some kind of crossover SUV thing."

Ty's blood chilled. How the hell had he missed that vehicle? Maybe Neil was right; maybe he wasn't fully recovered yet from his gunshot wound.

"That's the driver I'm waiting for to return to his vehicle, so I can see if it's just a coincidence he headed to town when we did," Neil explained. "But you grabbed me, so I probably missed him."

"I hope you did," Ty replied. Because then that meant it had just been a coincidence.

If the person was still here—somewhere—then there was a chance that he was the one after Neil and his ex-wife.

"Where's Elise?" he asked.

"She's in my locked SUV. She's safe," Neil said, as if trying to reassure himself.

"And she would stay there?" Ty asked—because he knew his former sister-in-law. She was as independent and stubborn as Neil was, which was probably why they hadn't been able to make their marriage work.

Neil tensed, probably with fear, because he knew Elise far better than Ty did. So why the hell would he have left her in the SUV in the first place? He had to know that she wasn't going to stay there.

Why hadn't he returned yet? He'd promised he was only going to take a quick look around and then come back to his vehicle, back to her.

Elise had been waiting a few years for that to happen, though, for him to come and beg for her forgiveness, to beg her to give them another chance. Sure, he'd recently been proposing, but that was only because of the baby. She'd wanted him to come back for her—for *them*—not out of some archaic sense of obligation. But because he loved her and that she was enough for him.

Now she just wanted him back in the damn SUV—safe—with her.

"Neil…" she murmured.

It had been too long. She needed to do something. She reached inside her purse for her cell. She needed to call his sister, to tell Jordana that he'd done it again—he'd put himself in danger.

But was he in danger?

She hadn't heard any gunshots or the blasts of any explosions.

Maybe he'd found the person who'd followed them off his street, and he was having a friendly conversation with a neighbor. The neighbor was sure to have been curious about all the cop cars in Neil's driveway.

With a weary sigh, she pushed open the passenger's door and stepped onto the sidewalk. A dull ache throbbed in her feet. Not only were the heels too high, but the boots had gotten too tight. Maybe swollen feet were another side effect of pregnancy, like the all-day nausea. Or maybe the swelling was an effect of all the fries she'd eaten off Neil's plate.

How far had Neil gone? He hadn't told her which vehicle he'd thought had followed them. And she hadn't noticed it at all. Not that she'd been looking for one; she wasn't used to someone trying to kill her.

And she didn't intend to get used to it. She intended to find out who was trying to kill them.

Not by trying to confront or trap them like Neil, but by going through old records from their former partnership. Despite what he'd said in the diner, she knew he had no intention of leaving the investigation to his sister. Hell, he couldn't even legally let Jordana go through their case files—not without violating lawyer-client confidentiality.

"Neil?" she called out as she glanced up and down the sidewalk. Other people walked along, some with shopping bags dangling from their gloved hands, some with dog leashes as they walked their pets. But she didn't catch a glimpse of Neil's lean body, of his dark hair, of his neatly trimmed beard.

Where was he? Which way had he even gone?

The guy at the Christmas tree lot could have seen him. From the big tip Neil had given him, the guy would remember him for certain. Since the lot was across the street, she stepped off the sidewalk between two vehicles parked at the curb.

While she waited for a break in the slow-moving traffic, a strange sensation rushed over her, like she could feel someone watching her.

Neil?

Was he close?

He had to be. A protective as he'd been of her—probably because of her pregnancy as much as their would-be killer—he wouldn't have gone that far away from her. He probably wouldn't have gotten talking to someone and forgotten all about her, either.

Had something happened to him?

Maybe she just needed to call Jordana. Better that she had the detective come over a false alarm than wait too long to get help for Neil.

First she would talk to the Christmas tree seller, though. Hopefully the young man had seen Neil and knew what had happened to him.

Finally the traffic cleared. As she headed across the four lanes toward the lot, lights flashed on and one of the vehicles at the curb pulled into the street.

Then an engine revved and those lights bore down on her as the vehicle headed directly toward her. With it gaining speed after shifting into Drive, she had only moments to react, to run...

And Elise was not a runner—especially not in those damn high-heel boots. But if she didn't move, she was going to get struck.

Hard.

Chapter 15

Worried about Elise, Neil had hurried out of the alley to make sure that she was safe and still locked inside his SUV. But before he could get to his vehicle, he had to pass the one he'd been watching when he'd stepped into the alley.

It was still there, and now there was someone behind the wheel, clad in a hoodie pulled tight around his face, just like the intruder had been. Of course, many people owned dark hoodies, so it might not have been the same person. But Neil damn well intended to find out.

The driver must have noticed him approaching, because the lights suddenly flashed on and the engine revved to life. In that flash of light, Neil noticed the woman starting across the street.

Elise.

The headlamps illuminated her face, which was white with fear. She saw the vehicle headed toward her. Neil started running, but he doubted he would reach her in time. The vehicle was too close.

And Elise, who hated to run, did not. As the vehicle bore down on her, she dove back toward the sidewalk she'd stepped off and onto the hood of one of the vehicles parked against the curb.

The brakes on the SUV squealed as the driver swerved back to the right and into the side of the vehicle whose hood Elise was sprawled on. Her body limp as a ragdoll, she tumbled off the hood and onto the sidewalk, and the SUV sped away.

Despite the horror gripping him, Neil moved. Running to where she lay on the sidewalk, he dropped to his knees next to her. Her long hair was tangled across her face, so he couldn't see it—couldn't see if her eyes were open—if she was unconscious or…

He couldn't even consider that—that she might be *gone*. Not Elise.

She had to be all right. He reached out, his hand shaking, to brush the tendrils of gold hair off her face.

A strong hand gripped his shoulder as Ty leaned down. "Is she all right? Elise?"

Her eyes opened then, and she stared up at them both. But her expression was blank, as if she was just too stunned—or too injured—to speak.

"Call 911!" Neil shouted at his brother, surprised that he could speak for the fear clogging his throat.

"Are you hurt?" Ty asked her again.

"Call!" Neil shouted. "And then go after that damn vehicle! Catch him!"

"You don't think it was an accident?" Ty asked. But at least he had his cell out.

"That was the vehicle that followed us, that was the intruder from her condo earlier this evening." He was sure of it now, after the man had tried to kill her.

Had he been successful?

Her eyes were open, but she still hadn't spoken. And her stare was so vacant.

"Elise?" he called to her, his voice cracking with the emotion overwhelming him. He wasn't used to her not speaking to him. As angry as they'd gotten at each other during their marriage and partnership, they had never given each other the silent treatment.

Maybe they should have.

At least, he should have. Because when he got upset and hurt, he said things he didn't mean —like he wanted a divorce. He hadn't really wanted to end their marriage. He hadn't ever wanted that. But he hadn't wanted to wind up like his parents either, just sharing a house and nothing else.

"Elise?"

His hand shaking, he cupped her cheek. Her skin was so cold. He wanted to lift her up from the concrete sidewalk, but he didn't dare move her—in case something was broken, or she had internal injuries. Or a serious head wound.

He moved his hand from her cheek to the back of her head. Her hair was cold, too, and silky and dry. She wasn't bleeding. But that only meant that she didn't have an open wound.

He glanced up to look for his brother. But Ty must have left to pursue the vehicle like he'd told him to.

Had he called 911 like he'd asked?

He couldn't hear any sirens, nothing but the murmurs of the people who stood nearby, watching them with curiosity and concern. "Did anyone call 911?" he asked.

A few of them nodded.

And a breath eased out between his lips. So even if Ty hadn't called, help was still on the way. But would it get here soon enough?

Elise still hadn't spoken. Still hadn't moved.

Tears of fear and frustration stung his eyes. If only he hadn't left her alone.

If only he'd made certain she was safe.

"I'm so sorry," he murmured.

He had failed her. He had failed *them*.

Again.

She was afraid to move. Afraid to speak.

Afraid that she'd done something to hurt the baby.

That was probably why Neil was so upset. She could hear the fear and concern in his voice. But when he leaned back and his handsome face was no longer just a shadow to her, she saw everything else: the guilt, the pain.

His blue eyes were dark with it, his handsome face contorted into a grimace of it. He was in far more pain than she was.

Hell, she wasn't hurting at all. She was just stunned.

So stunned that it had happened, that she had managed to jump through the air like she had. But her instincts had warned her that if she continued to cross the road, the SUV would have pursued her. By jumping back toward the sidewalk, instead, toward the protection of the other parked cars, she'd had a chance.

For herself...

For her baby...

That was why she was lying so still on the concrete. She was waiting for the pain. For the loss.

Wasn't she supposed to be in pain? Bleeding?

But she felt nothing except concern for Neil. So finally she moved, reaching up to cover his hand that cupped her face. "I'm okay," she assured him.

He leaned closer. "Oh my God, you scared the hell out of me! I thought you..." His deep voice cracked with emotion. "You weren't talking or moving."

"I just had to catch my breath," she murmured, but she still wasn't able to draw in a deep one, not with how awkwardly she was lying on the sidewalk. "Although, I'm sure my not talking scared the crap out of you." She managed a chuckle.

And so did he. "It did. You've never not spoken to me."

And there had been times that she shouldn't have, because maybe he would have listened more to her silence than he had the things she'd told him, like she just needed time before starting a family.

"I'm sure you enjoyed my not talking," she said. "But I'm fine now." She reached out with her other hand and grasped his shoulder, so she could pull herself up.

But he pushed her back gently. "Don't move," he told her. "You might be hurt worse than you realize."

She'd lain there motionless partly to wait for the shock to wear off, so that she could assess whether or not she had any injuries. She might be sore tomorrow, but at the moment she was just cold. And lying on the sidewalk wasn't warming her up any.

"I'm fine," she insisted. "Nothing hurts."

"You might be fine," he said. "But what about the baby?"

And suddenly something hurt—as pain stabbed her heart. Of course. The baby was all he cared about.

But because she was concerned, too, she lay back on the sidewalk and jerked her hands away from him. Her eyes stung with emotion, and she quickly closed them to hold in the threatening tears. She'd already cried too many of them over Neil Colton.

"Elise?" The concern was back in his voice, but now she knew it wasn't for her.

She just shook her head.

He might have said something else, but sirens from the arriving emergency vehicles drowned him out. Not that it mattered.

She doubted that he was ever going to say what she wanted to hear. That he loved her.

She knew that if she lost this baby, then she'd lost Neil, too. He wasn't going to want to marry her. Hell, he probably wasn't even going to want to see her again.

She kept her eyes closed so she couldn't see him. And so she couldn't shed the tears that threatened to overwhelm her.

* * *

He glanced into the rearview mirror, watching for lights. Neil Colton hadn't been alone when he'd run out of wherever the hell he'd been hiding. While the lawyer had stayed behind, the other man had jumped into a truck.

He'd noticed the vehicle earlier on Colton's street. It had followed them, too. Was it following him now?

And who the hell was it? Had Colton hired security? He wouldn't put it past the spoiled rich kid.

Neil Colton had everything given to him from his daddy who ran the construction company. He probably didn't even have to work. But he had chosen to—and what a damn profession he'd chosen.

He worked at helping criminals get away with their crimes. And the mayor had worked right alongside him when she first came to Braxville. But she'd been too damn ambitious to stay in private practice.

Hell, she wasn't even a local and now she was running the place.

Until he'd run her down. She had to be dead. Or hurt very damn badly.

Either way, they were both suffering—she and Colton. But their suffering would never compare to his.

Chapter 16

What the hell had happened?

One minute Elise was touching him, almost comforting *him*, and the next she'd pulled away from him... physically and emotionally.

Was she worried about the baby? Was that the reason?

Neil had never been as relieved to hear sirens as he'd been when the ambulance had arrived. But when he started to climb inside the back with her, she'd held up a hand in protest.

"Stay here," she said. "File the report. You saw more than I did."

He should have. He should have made note of the license plate, but all he'd focused on was Elise, flying through the air and then tumbling off onto the concrete. His gut clenched with the horror he'd felt watching that, watching her while being so damn helpless to protect her.

Maybe that was why she'd withdrawn. Maybe she was angry with him. And he couldn't blame her. He was so damn mad at himself.

"I want to go with you," he said.

"Meet me at the hospital," she said. "You need your vehicle anyway."

It was clear that Elise didn't want him riding in the ambulance with her.

She even urged the EMT to close the doors and drive away. Was she worried about the baby? Was she scared that she was losing it?

Desperate to make sure that she and the baby were all right, he headed toward his SUV, but he hadn't made it more than a few steps before a hand on his arm jerked him to a stop. He whirled toward Detective Carpenter.

"We need your statement," Reese said.

Neil shook his head. "Not now."

Not when he could be losing Elise all over again. Because if she lost the baby, he had no chance of getting her back. She'd proved the past three years that she didn't need him. Hell, that she did even better on her own.

"Neil," his sister rushed up to join them now. "Is Elise okay?"

He shrugged. "I don't know. That's why I have to go."

Her brow furrowed. "Why didn't you go with her?"

Because she hadn't wanted him to...

"I—I..."

"Do you want me to drive you?" she asked.

"Then we can take your report on the ride," Carpenter added.

He shook his head. "No. I need my vehicle. And I didn't see anything." He turned back to Jordana. "Ask your other brother. The one you asked to follow me and didn't think to inform me about."

She glanced around. "Where is Ty?"

"I think he took off after the hit-and-run driver," Neil said.

"You think that's all this was?" Reese asked. "An accident? Someone who had too much to drink that nearly struck her?"

"No. It was the same guy I saw in her condo."

"I thought you didn't get a good look at him," Jordana said, her eyes narrowed with suspicion.

"I didn't—not with the hoodie pulled around his face, but it was the same guy." He was certain of it. Now he just had to be certain that Elise was truly all right. "Talk to Ty. I have to go."

He only hoped that when he got to the hospital he wouldn't be too late.

That Elise hadn't lost their child...

Lilly paced the ambulance bay, but even as fast as she walked, she couldn't escape the fear that gripped her. Fear for Neil, for Elise and for the grandchild she was going to have—as long as Elise hadn't been hurt too badly.

Poor Elise...

"The EMT said she'd been struck by a car?" she

asked for confirmation from the ER resident who leaned against the wall behind her, smoking.

Why would a health professional neglect his own health? She resisted the urge to lecture, barely, reminding herself that she wasn't this young man's mother.

The guy nodded. "Yeah, hit-and-run."

Her stomach flipped, making her feel as nauseated as if she was pregnant, too. The explosion and now this.

What was going on? Why was someone after Neil and Elise? Or was the mayor the real target?

"Only a female was injured?" she asked.

The guy nodded.

"Was she alone?"

He shrugged. "I don't know," he replied, irritation sharpening his voice. "I wasn't there."

Now she really wanted to lecture him about common courtesy as well as his severely lacking bedside manner. And as part of the training and development team at the hospital, that was her place. But before she could open her mouth to make any comment, the ambulance sped into the bay.

The young resident finally moved, tossing down his cigarette before helping the EMTs open the back doors. Lilly, despite all her years of nursing experience, froze for a moment. It didn't matter that Elise was no longer her daughter-in-law; she loved that young woman like she was one of her daughters.

And the baby…

She sucked in a breath as the EMTs pulled out the gurney, and along with the resident, wheeled Elise toward the open doors to the emergency room. Lilly rushed along beside it. "Are you all right?"

Tears trailed down Elise's cheeks, and she shook her head.

Lilly glanced toward the paramedics. "How badly is she hurt?"

"She says she's fine," the female EMT remarked. "She's just worried about her pregnancy."

"She's pregnant?" the resident asked.

"Not more than four weeks," Lilly replied.

"First trimester," the resident murmured, then directed his attention toward the EMTs. "Any signs of miscarriage?"

"No bleeding and she has no pain," one of the EMTs replied. "She doesn't have any cuts or even apparent bruising. Looks like she was damn lucky."

"A car ran her down, though," Lilly reminded them.

"I jumped," Elise said. "I jumped out of the way— onto another car. It hit that one and knocked me off onto the sidewalk." Lying on the gurney, she wrapped her arms around her stomach, as if trying to hold the baby inside her.

And Lilly's heart broke at the fear and loss on the young woman's face. She reached out and squeezed one of Elise's arms. "You're going to be fine," she said. "And that's all that matters."

Elise shook her head. "Your son doesn't think so. To him, the baby is all that matters."

Lilly gasped. Neil could be such an idiot. What had he said? What had he done?

"I don't want him in the exam room," Elise said.

"Don't let him in." She reached out and grasped Lilly's arm now, her grip reassuringly strong but that might have been the strength of the desperation on her face. She reminded Lilly, "You told me to do what I want. I don't want him in there."

"Okay…" Lilly said and swallowed hard. "Will it be all right if I check on you?"

Elise grasped her arm more tightly. "I want you with me." More tears rolled down her face. "If it's okay with you."

Lilly knew how hard it was for Elise to ask for help. She was as strong and fiercely independent as every one of Lilly's biological children. "I want to be there."

The resident glanced at her as she ran alongside the gurney. Once they'd rolled Elise into an open bay of the ER, he asked, "You got this? You'll get her ready for exam?"

She nodded. "Of course." She waited until he and the paramedics stepped out before she pulled the curtain closed. Then she helped Elise out of her dress and into a gown.

The EMTs had not done a very thorough evaluation of Elise. Bruises were already beginning to darken the skin on the young woman's shoulder, hip and back.

Her heart aching over the injuries, she murmured, "You're going to be sore tomorrow."

It was clear that Elise was hurting already, though. Emotionally.

Without waiting for the resident's orders, Lilly dragged over the ultrasound machine. She wanted to check on her grandchild nearly as much as Elise wanted her to, but before she could even turn on the machine, the resident stepped back into the area.

"I thought you said she was only a month along," he said. "You're not going to be able to tell if she miscarried with that."

"Dr. Thiel did a transvaginal ultrasound when Ms. Willis was in the ER last night."

"Last night?" the resident asked. "What's going on?" He examined Elise now, finding the bruises the paramedic had missed. "Is a partner abusing you?"

At the thought of her son harming the woman he obviously still loved, Lilly gasped.

But Elise's lips curved into a slight smile of amusement. "No. I'm in danger, though."

"There are women's shelters—"

"Not that way," Elise assured him. "Somebody is trying to kill me."

"Yes, and you need to report him—"

"I would," Elise interjected. "If I had a clue who it was. Can you please just check, like the other doctor did, to see if that weird little bubble shows up yet?"

The doctor's brow creased with confusion. Either he was struggling to believe she didn't know who hurt her, or he didn't follow what she was talking about.

"The gestational sac," Lilly said. "That's what she wants to see." She wasn't the only one.

But before the doctor had a chance to comply with Elise's request, another nurse pulled the curtain aside to say, "Lilly, your son's here and he's trying to come back—"

"No!" Elise said.

"Is he the one?" the doctor asked. "The one who's hurting you?"

Elise shook her head. "Not like that…"

Not like that. But he was hurting her. And Lilly hated that—hated that Neil couldn't make things right between them again. But she knew why.

He was too damn much like his father.

"I'll handle it," Lilly assured her former daughter-in-law, and she headed out to the waiting room where Neil was yelling at a nervous security guard. Her son appeared to be fine except for the anger flushing his face and making his eyes glow brightly.

"I want to see my wife!" he shouted. "The ambulance just brought her in. I need to be with her!"

"You should have thought about that before you divorced her," Lilly admonished him.

Neil's mouth fell open as if Lilly had slapped him. Maybe she should have—not now but when he'd made such a stupid decision. But she'd never been one of those mothers who meddled in her children's lives. With the mistakes she'd made, she'd never felt qualified to give out advice.

"Mom?" Neil finally remarked questioningly, as if he wasn't sure he recognized her.

She drew in a deep breath to calm herself; she was nearly as angry as he was, as he'd been. Now he just stood there, waiting, as if expecting the worst.

"Is she right?" Lilly asked. "Is the baby all you care about?"

The color faded from his face now, leaving it starkly white. "Is that what she thinks?"

"What else would she think after what you did." She shook her head. "You screwed up once with her. She must have given you a second chance or you wouldn't have conceived that baby in the first place, but you're obviously messing that up, too." She'd never been as disappointed in one of her children as she was now.

"I didn't run her down," Neil said, as if she was blaming him for that.

Then she realized he was blaming himself. Her anger drained away, and she approached him, hugging him tightly. "I know. You would never hurt her physically." No matter what the ER resident might suspect now. "But emotionally, you have to be more careful. Elise isn't as tough as she wants everyone to think she is."

Lilly knew because she was the same way herself. She had never been as strong as she'd wanted to be. She'd once been very, very weak.

Tears stung her eyes, but she blinked them back. She couldn't fix what she'd done. But there was still time for Neil—if he was careful.

"Be patient for once," she told him. "Don't fight to get your way like you've always done." As a triplet, he'd probably felt like he'd had to, but as a husband...

But he wasn't a husband anymore.

"She doesn't want me back there, does she?" Neil asked, his shoulders slumping.

Her mother's heart ached for him, but she was also a nurse with a patient that was very special to her. "No."

"Can you tell me if she mis—"

"No," she said. "Wait for Elise." She hugged him again and then stepped back and repeated the advice she should have given him a couple of years ago, before the divorce. "Wait for Elise."

It was what he should have done last time but hadn't. Would he take her advice? Or would he once again push too hard and lose the woman he loved?

Of course—with someone trying to kill her—he might lose Elise another way—a way in which he would never be able to get her back.

She was heartbroken. But she wasn't heartless.

Not long after Lilly left to get rid of her son, Elise called another nurse over to allow him to see her and their child. She stared so intently at the ultrasound screen, at that little bubble that was the developing baby, that she didn't notice the curtain had been opened… until she heard Neil's gasp.

She turned toward him, and the look on his face… The longing, the love, as he stared at that screen. She probably stared at him the same way—with the same love and longing. If only he had ever looked at her like that. While love for him overwhelmed her, she also felt a pang of jealousy, of regret.

A few years ago she hadn't understood why he'd wanted so badly to start their family, especially as they'd still been getting their practice going at the time. But now she knew how much it meant to him to be a father. How much the baby meant to him.

"That thing," she said, pointing toward the bubble. The doctor had removed the ultrasound wand but had left the image up on the screen—at her request. "That's what they call the gestational sac. It's still there, so the baby is still there, too."

He nodded and turned his attention to her then. "What about you? Are you all right?"

"Yes," she said. But it was a lie.

"Elise, I don't know why you're upset with me."

That was the problem; he had no idea.

"I'm sorry that I wasn't there when that SUV came after you," he said. "I was talking to Ty, and I—I shouldn't have let him distract me. I should have been protecting you. I promise that I'll do that now...if you'll come home with me. I'll take care of you now."

"No." She shook her head. "I can't stay with you." Because it would only make it harder for her to leave again once their would-be killer was caught.

Chapter 17

Neil couldn't stop staring at Elise as she studied the ultrasound image. He had no idea what she was looking at. There were only fuzzy bubbles on the screen. But he could easily determine that the look on Elise's face was a combination of concern and love.

She loved their baby already. Would she ever love him again? Or had he completely blown it with her?

The young doctor who'd joined them seconds ago looked at Neil with suspicion. "A car really almost ran her over?" he asked.

Neil nodded. "But she jumped out of the way before it hit her."

The doctor's eyes narrowed, but he remarked, "That must have been frightening. Did they catch the guy?"

"I hope so," he said.

Had Ty caught him? He hoped like hell that he had, that this was all over, but then he knew that Elise would insist on returning to her condo despite its current messy state. And a pang of regret struck him. He silently cursed his own selfishness.

"If you'll be safe, you can go home," the doctor told her.

"I'll make sure she is," Neil vowed.

The doctor spared him a skeptical glance before turning back to Elise. "You're going to be sore tomorrow. I would prescribe painkillers if you weren't pregnant."

"I'll be fine," Elise assured him, with her hand sliding protectively over her stomach.

"You can ice the bruises," he advised, "and take low-dose aspirin as needed."

"Thank you, Doctor," she said.

The resident pulled the curtain aside and slipped out of the space, leaving them alone together.

Elise kept staring at that screen. She wouldn't look at him, hadn't looked at him since he had first joined her in the ER.

"Why are you so angry with me?" he asked.

She shook her head. "I'm not. I'm just…" She sighed. "I'm tired, Neil."

"Then let me take you home," he urged.

She shook her head again.

"You can't go back to your condo," he said. "It isn't safe."

"Maybe they caught him," she said hopefully. "My phone's been ringing, but I haven't picked it up."

It had probably been Detective Carpenter either calling to question her or update her. She was the mayor, so the police department was more likely to keep her apprised of the investigation than they were him.

He sighed. "I hope he was caught." He didn't want them or anyone else in danger because of this maniac— even if it meant she would be able to return to her condo. "But even if they have, your place is a mess. You need rest. Stay with me tonight."

She uttered a heavy sigh and nodded. "Just for tonight."

The tension inside him didn't ease any. He wanted her home with him, but not just for one night.

"Elise! Elise!"

Neil shouted her name, panic in his voice. The panic drew her to the top of the steps. "I'm up here," she called down to him.

He appeared at the foot of the staircase, her bags clutched in his hands. "Why?"

"I'm sleeping up here," she informed him.

"But the doctor said you would be sore," he reminded her. "You should be on the main floor—in our bedroom."

"Yours," she reminded him. "It's your bedroom." And she'd already spent too much time in it recently.

"Elise—"

"The doctor said I need rest," she interrupted. "So stop arguing with me and let me go to sleep."

He snapped his mouth shut and headed up the stairs with her bags. And she nearly laughed. It had to be killing him not to argue with her. But before he'd started calling for her, she'd heard him arguing with someone else. So maybe he'd gotten his fix for the night.

"Who were you talking to a little bit ago?" she asked. And had he been on the phone or had someone been at the door? She hadn't heard the doorbell, but the person could have intercepted him when he'd gone outside to retrieve the suitcases from her vehicle.

"It sounded like a female," she added, and heat flushed her face as she realized she sounded like a jealous wife. Since she was no longer his wife, she had no right to that jealousy—not even because she was carrying his child.

That night…

And last night…

Those had been aberrations. Errors in judgment. Because—despite his proposals—he had to know that they wouldn't be able to sustain a relationship, let alone a marriage. They'd already failed once. Why try again?

Elise wanted more for her child than she had. Two parents would be nice. But that didn't mean she had to be married to the baby's father—just that he had to be involved.

Would he?

Or would he be the kind of father he'd had? Always working and never around? That was one of the reasons she'd wanted to wait before starting their family. She hadn't wanted to be solely responsible for raising the baby like her mother had been, like Lilly had essentially been, despite having Fitz as a husband.

Neil remained silent as he carried her bags into the

guest room, and she realized he was reluctant to tell her who he'd been talking to. Was he seeing someone?

Last month—when they'd succumbed to passion—he'd told her no. But that had been four weeks ago. A lot could have happened since then.

He lifted her suitcases onto the dresser then turned back toward her. "It was Jordana."

"You were arguing with her," she said. "So I guess they didn't find the person who tried to run me down."

He shook his head. "And she wanted to interview you. That's why she showed up here, but I told her it would have to wait until you had some sleep."

"It would be a waste of her time anyway," Elise said. "I didn't see him. I didn't even see the vehicle. The first thing I saw were the lights when they came on bright, blinding me." She shuddered as she remembered the fear, being frozen for a moment before finally moving. She'd thought she was going to die.

Strong arms closed around her as Neil pulled her into an embrace. Maybe he'd meant it to be comforting, but when their bodies touched, hers reacted to the closeness of his. Her skin tingled, and her pulse quickened.

She wanted to link her arms around his neck and pull his head down for her kiss. She wanted to be with him—completely—with him inside her, filling her. But even then, she wouldn't be truly complete…because there would always be the ache yawning inside her as her heart yearned for his love—his unconditional love.

She stepped back out of his loose embrace. "I'm really tired," she murmured.

She really was and not just because of the long, exhausting day she'd had. She was tired of wanting something she would never have.

And even if he claimed to love her, she would never trust it. Not after their divorce.

They needed to find out whoever was after them, so that the threat against them was over and that they could figure out how to manage the future, raising a child together without being together.

But first they had to make sure they had a future, that the man trying to kill them was identified and brought to justice.

Jordana shook her head, disgusted with her brother's stubbornness. "You'd think he would want to do everything possible to try to find out who the hell is after him and Elise," she muttered at Neil's closed front door.

But she knew better than to continue arguing with the consummate arguer. So she walked away from the house to where her partner leaned against the passenger's side of their unmarked car.

"He won't let us interview her?" Reese asked, then covered his mouth as a yawn escaped with his question.

"I know it's late," Jordana said. Or early, actually as the sky was already beginning to lighten with dawn's approach. "But he's being overprotective."

"Says the woman who enlisted the security expert to follow them around," Reese teased.

She snorted derisively. "A lot of good that did me."

"Hey!" Ty exclaimed in protest of her complaint. He leaned against the side of his truck, which was parked in front of the Braxville PD vehicle. "Once I got to town, which unfortunately was after he tried confronting the intruder at Elise's place, I was with Neil, protecting him—just like you asked me to."

"I know. I know." Jordana sighed. "I'm just worried about him."

"I'm more worried about Elise," Ty said.

She tensed. "Why? You think she's the real target?"

"I think if something happens to her, it'll kill Neil," Ty said. "So keeping her safe should probably be our first priority."

"Too damn bad you didn't catch the guy who tried running her down."

"I got you a plate number," Ty said defensively.

Too defensively.

Jordana knew that he was pissed at himself for not catching the guy.

"The license plate number of a vehicle reported stolen earlier today," Reese said. "It doesn't lead us anywhere."

"We'll figure out who's trying to kill them," Jordana said.

They had to…

"You're sure it's not Dex?" Ty asked.

After the guy had shot him, it was no wonder Ty would harbor a grudge against him. Jordana wasn't happy with their father's business partner, either.

She shook her head, though. "Neil and Elise think it's probably something to do with the time they were in practice together."

"They actually agreed on something?" Ty asked.

Jordana chuckled. "Yeah."

"You want me to protect both of them from this would-be killer?" Ty asked. "But the real question is who's going to protect them from each other?"

Chapter 18

Despite not having a case and refusing to take on any new clients, Neil had spent the entire day in the office, going through old files. Mostly he'd packed up the ones on which he'd worked with Elise. And he'd remembered how it had been to work with her, to live with her, to make love with her.

That was all he'd spent the previous night imagining… while he'd slept alone in their bed and she'd spent the night in the guest room upstairs. Hopefully she'd gotten some rest—because he sure as hell hadn't.

Which, unfortunately, hadn't done anything for his temper. So when he arrived at City Hall to pick up Elise at the end of what had seemed like an interminably long day, he was in no mood to confront slimy Jeremy again. But as Neil was heading toward Elise's office, Jeremy was leaving it. The guy, with his slicked-back blond hair and phony tan, pulled her door shut and stood in front of it, as if barring Neil entrance to it. To her...

Neil furrowed his brow and stared at the other man. "What are you doing, Jerry?" he asked, impatient to get the man out of his way and to get Elise home—where she would be safe.

Elise thought she was safe here because of the security at City Hall, and Neil's detective sister and security brother had concurred. But he wasn't as convinced, mostly because of her deputy mayor.

"What are *you* doing?" Jeremy asked. "You divorced her. Why don't you leave her the hell alone?"

"Why don't you mind your own damn business?" Neil asked.

"Elise is my business," Jeremy insisted.

Neil snorted. "I'm sure you'd like to think that, but you're delusional if you think you're anything more to her than her deputy mayor."

"I'm her friend," Jeremy said. "A friend who's worried that you're putting her in danger."

"I'm trying to keep her safe," Neil said in his defense, though doubt niggled at him. Was he the reason she was in danger?

Jeremy snorted now. "If you really wanted to keep her safe, you would stay the hell away from her. You and your family has been involved in every bad thing to happen to Braxville over the past several months." He snorted again. "Hell, probably years. Who knows what the health department's going to find out about your father's business?"

Nerves tightened Neil's stomach. What was going to be discovered in the investigation? He'd been wondering that himself. But he was almost afraid of what the truth might be.

Of how involved his father was in everything.

"Markus Dexter had been his business partner for years," Jeremy continued. "How the hell could he not know the man's a killer?"

"Alleged killer," Neil said, the lawyer in him automatically making the correction.

"Yeah, because innocent men flee to avoid prosecution," Jeremy scoffed.

Neil sighed. "I'm not saying he's innocent. I just don't think he's the one going after Elise."

"So you're saying the attempts on her life have nothing to do with you?" Jeremy asked, his voice thick with disgust.

Neil wished he could say that, but he shook his head. "I don't know, Jeremy," he admitted. "Maybe these attempts on our lives have been made by someone who's frustrated that no matter how much he wants Elise, he'll never be able to have her—that she will always belong with me instead. You know how some stalkers get. If they can't have the object of their affection, no one else can."

Jeremy's face flushed, and his eyes bulged with fury. "I don't know what the hell you're insinuating."

"You know exactly what I'm insinuating," Neil said. That was why Jeremy was so damn mad—that Neil knew exactly how the man felt about his boss and that it was futile for him to have those feelings.

"You're a son of a bitch!" Jeremy hurled the insult at him and then stepped closer, as if he was about to hurl his fists, as well.

Ty might have thought he didn't need to trail Neil inside City Hall—that the security would eliminate any threat to his and Elise's safety. But Neil wasn't so damn sure...

Jeremy was bigger than he was, like the intruder at Elise's condo. And like the intruder, he was also fast. He swung his fist before Neil even had a chance to duck. The blow knocked him back and released his fury. He came back swinging.

Weary from another sleepless night, Elise hadn't jumped up from her desk when she first heard the heated confrontation between the two men outside her office door. She had little energy to deal with a show of male testosterone.

But when the insults began, she rose from her chair and headed around her desk. She'd just pulled open the door when the first fist landed—squarely on Neil's square jaw. Neil, being Neil, couldn't walk away from a fight. So he swung back, knocking Jeremy toward her. She stepped back, out of the way, as he struck the door jamb near her.

"Oh my God, Elise!" Neil exclaimed. "Did he hit you?"

"I didn't hit her," Jeremy said. "You almost did."

"Did I?" Neil asked with concern.

"No, I'm fine," she said, but it had been too close for

her comfort. Fury erupted. "But what the hell is wrong with the two of you?"

She glanced from one to the other. Neil's face had gone pale but for a slight red mark on one cheek, while Jeremy's eye was already swelling, and for once his slickly gelled blond hair was mussed.

"I'm sorry, Elise." Jeremy was the first to apologize. "But this guy wasn't ever good for you, and now he and his troublesome family are going to get you killed. I can't just stand by and say nothing when you're in danger."

Neil cursed, and the color rushed back into his face. But he didn't argue now.

"I appreciate your concern, Jeremy," she said with sincerity. She was actually impressed that he'd taken on Neil like he had. She hadn't believed he had the guts. "But I don't believe Neil or his family is at fault for the recent attempts on my life."

At least not solely. She had probably had some part in it, too, from back when they'd shared their practice. She wasn't about to share that with Jeremy, though. While she was impressed with his show of bravery, she still didn't entirely trust him. He enjoyed talking to the press a little too much, and she didn't want to give him fodder for the media. It was bad enough she'd had to dodge them on her way into the office again that morning.

Apparently they had police radio scanners and had heard about her being nearly run down the night before. After the explosion the night before that, most had suspected—rightfully—that the hit-and-run had been no accident, either.

If Jeremy had been responsible for those nonaccidents, though, why would he blame and attack Neil? Just to deflect suspicion? While she knew he was ambitious, she doubted he was that diabolical.

But then he was a politician.

So was she, though. But she was much too straightforward to be diabolical, no matter what her former father-in-law believed of her.

"How can you not think he or his family have anything to do with the attempts on your life?" Jeremy asked, clearly dumbfounded and maybe even a little disappointed with her.

"I know them better than you do," she pointed out.

"I know that they're going to hurt you," Jeremy said. "If not physically, then politically. Nobody's going to vote for anybody that has anything to do with a Colton. You even risk a recall if you continue to associate with them."

A recall...

Had he started the process? Getting her recalled so that he could take her job?

Bristling with defensiveness, Neil interjected, "You don't know—"

"Stop!" She tightened her grip on his arm, tempted to shake some sense—or at least some patience—into him. But that was something she'd never been able to get from him: patience.

"How can you not think he's capable of violence?" Jeremy asked.

She smiled at the irony, while Neil bristled even more.

"You threw the first punch!"

"I was protecting her," Jeremy said in his defense.

Elise's patience ran out now. "Enough! Jeremy, I appreciate your concern, but you need to let me handle my own life." She pointed toward the door.

"I just want to make sure you have a life," Jeremy said, but he headed to the door, as if realizing she wasn't going to listen to him in regard to Neil.

She hoped he didn't take it personally. She rarely listened to herself when it came to Neil…or she wouldn't be pregnant right now. She wouldn't be staying with him in the house they'd designed together. But because she was pregnant—and in danger—she would stay with him until they discovered who was after them.

"I thought he'd never leave," Neil murmured.

She turned toward him and shook her head in disgust. "What the hell is wrong with you?"

"What do you mean?" Neil asked. "He started it."

"Because he was protecting me," she said. "What's your excuse?"

"I'm protecting you, too," Neil insisted.

She snorted. "You weren't protecting me, then. You two were acting like a couple little boys posturing on the playground. And I felt like your mom having to break you apart."

His mouth curved into a slight, sexy grin. "That's good practice for you, then," he said. "In case we have a son."

Her heart warmed. A son…

She wouldn't care if they had a boy or a girl, though. She just wanted the baby to be healthy. "Girls can fight, too," she reminded him.

He chuckled. "You don't have to tell me," he said. "I have sisters." His grin slipped away. "I don't want this child to be an only child. I'd like for him to have sisters and brothers, Elise. Please won't you just accept—"

She reached out and pressed her fingers over his lips. "No. You promised you'd stop pressuring me."

"Elise…" He sighed, and his breath brushed across her fingertips, making her skin tingle.

She wanted to say yes, but she could only do that if she truly believed that Neil loved her—just her. And she would never believe that now.

"Is it because you're worried about what Jeremy brought up?" he asked, his lips moving against her skin.

She pulled her hand away from his mouth, from his damn handsome face. "What?"

"A recall. The Coltons hurting your career."

She snorted again. "No. I'm not worried about that. And I'm not worried about this baby being an only child. I'm an only child," she reminded him. "And I think I turned out fine. I'm not brawling in City Hall like you are. So maybe having siblings to fight with isn't all you think it is."

"That's not the reason I was fighting with Jeremy. I have had my suspicions about your deputy mayor for a while now," he replied.

She had, too, but she wasn't about to admit that to Neil. "I thought we both agreed that whoever is after us must have something to do with a case we worked on together."

He shrugged. "That makes the most sense."

"So we're going to the office to look through those now?" she asked.

He shook his head. "I packed them up and have them with me. We can go through them at home."

Home…

She swallowed a groan. She was going to start thinking of it that way again, too, if she kept going back there with him. They had to find and stop the person trying to kill them, so that she could go back to her condo. So that she could get the distance from Neil that she so desperately needed, or she might just accept his proposal.

He had to be careful now—because he wasn't the only one watching them. There was the man in the truck, the man who had come close to catching him the night before. He'd ditched that stolen SUV, though, and had rented a vehicle.

He wasn't going to try to run them down again…or even off the road. They'd driven separately to their offices this morning, and while Colton had joined her at City Hall and walked her to the parking garage, they'd driven separately back to his house. It was there that they were together—in one place—and it was there that he would take them out.

Together…

Chapter 19

A dark shadow fell across Neil as he stepped into the foyer of his house. Only faint light shone from the glass of the front door, filtering through the branches of the tree leaning against it.

"No deliveries," Ty admonished him. "That just gives this damn stalker of yours an opportunity to make another attempt on your lives."

"It's just a Christmas tree," Neil said as he pulled open the front door. The tree fell against him, nearly knocking him down, the way Jeremy nearly had Elise when Neil had struck the man earlier. Guilt and regret weighed on him as heavily as the tree did.

He shouldn't have lost his temper like that. Shouldn't have risked Elise getting hurt.

Ty inspected the tree, then helped Neil carry it

into the house. Elise, after changing into an oversize sweater and leggings, stood on the staircase. Once the tree cleared the foyer, she rushed to close the front door.

That was the only reason she was here, he reminded himself, for the security. She wasn't here because she was coming home to stay. No matter how many times he asked her, she kept turning him down.

Was it possible that whatever she'd felt for him once was gone? But then why make love with him last month?

Elise was more in control than he was. She didn't indulge in casual encounters. She was too busy and too public a figure to take the risk. He needed to ask her more about that night. But not now...

Not with Ty in the house, helping him stand up the tree in the great room. "So you think it's safe?" Neil teased his brother.

Ty sighed. "Nothing about this assignment is safe."

"For you?" Neil asked. His brother had always been tough and fearless.

"For you," Ty said, and he nodded his head in the direction of Elise who was in the kitchen.

Elise was the greatest danger to Neil—to his heart, which she'd already broken once. He was willing to trust her with it again, though, if she would give him the chance.

"I'm safe, right?" Neil asked. "With your protection?"

"I can't watch you twenty-four seven," Ty said.

And he had his own life, his own love. Neil understood that. And he could see, much to his disgust, that his brother was so in love that it had made him goofy.

"I think Jordana overreacted bringing you into it," he said.

"I'm not sure she's reacting enough," Ty said. "You and the mayor, especially, need police protection around the clock until this killer is caught."

When Elise had first become mayor, she had turned down having a personal protection detail. Maybe she hadn't wanted the city to pay for it; maybe she hadn't wanted anyone to know everywhere she went and whom she saw, like him.

Ty pushed a hand through his hair. "But I need to be with Ashley." He grinned at just the thought of his new girlfriend. "So I'm going to call Jordana to bring in police protection."

Neil felt a pang of jealousy. Love was so simple for Ty—disgustingly simple. "You can go right now," Neil urged him. "We're inside. We're safe."

Ty narrowed his eyes and studied his face. "You're going to stay inside? You won't let anyone else in?"

"I'm not an idiot," Neil said. And he hated how often he had to remind his older siblings of that fact.

Ty glanced at Elise again.

Was that why his family doubted his judgment? Because he'd divorced her? He couldn't blame them over that; it was the stupidest mistake he'd ever made.

But he'd really believed that they would never agree on one of the things that mattered most to him: family. And he hadn't wanted to wind up like his parents—with that chilly indifference between them.

He should have known then that he would never be able to be indifferent to Elise. He would always want her—even when she infuriated him. Maybe most when she infuriated him. He sighed.

And Ty chuckled. "Yeah, right, you know…"

Unfortunately he did. "I'll be careful," he promised his brother. "Go home to Ashley."

Ty's grin widened. "I'll make sure the police protection is on its way then head out."

"Thanks for coming to help," Neil said. Then he hugged his brother, maybe a little too tightly given he was still healing from his gunshot wound.

Ty let out a grunt as he patted his back. "Stay safe." He waved at Elise. "You, too."

She smiled at her ex-brother-in-law. "Thank you, Ty," she said. "Are you sure you won't stay for dinner?"

Ty shook his head. "Hopefully I can get home in time to eat with Ashley," he said, hurrying toward the front door.

As he opened and closed it behind himself, a chill ran down Neil's spine. Maybe it was just that a cold wind had blown in from outside. Or maybe it was unease with being alone.

But Jordana would send over protection, of course. They would be safe.

From whoever was trying to kill them.

Neil wasn't safe from Elise, though, not with him wanting her as much as he did. "You didn't have to cook," he told her as he joined her in the kitchen, where she was chopping up vegetables on a cutting board next to the stainless steel stove. She'd picked out the white cabinets, marble countertops and the fancy appliances, which he'd teased her about since she hadn't been very domestic back when they'd married.

After tossing the vegetables into a pan in which slices of chicken sizzled, she turned toward him and smiled. And as always, warmth flooded his heart.

"Don't worry," she said. "My cooking's gotten better since our divorce. I'm not going to poison you." She turned back to the stove and murmured, "At least not accidentally."

He chuckled. "I hope you're joking."

"I am," she said, her smile gone as she turned serious. "We're in enough danger. The stir-fry will be done in a little while. After we eat, we can start going through our old records."

Neil sighed. "I went through some of them today." He wanted a break now, a break from thinking about the past, so that he could focus on the future—a future he wanted to share with her and their baby. "How about we decorate the tree first? It looks so bare with nothing on it."

"It will survive," she said.

She obviously wasn't as convinced that they would.

"You teased me about not having any decorations up yet," he reminded her. "Pot…"

She smiled again, making that warmth flood his heart once again. "Calling me a hypocrite?"

"We'll need to get used to decorating for the holidays—with the baby coming," Neil persisted.

She sighed. "We'll be decorating separately, Neil. Not together."

"Why won't you even consider marrying me again?"

he asked, hurt that she wasn't at all tempted to accept his proposal. "Don't you have any feelings at all for me anymore?"

She had too many feelings for him. That was why she couldn't trust him with her heart again—not after he'd already broken it once.

"I once asked you that question," she reminded him as she blinked away the tears stinging her eyes.

She didn't dare look at his face, so she focused on the frying pan. The food was done, but she was reluctant to remove it from the burner. A low growl of hunger emanated from her stomach, though. And she knew she had to eat—for the baby.

That was the only reason she was here in this house, with its high-tech security system. For her child.

For the child who was all Neil had ever wanted. He hadn't wanted her. She nearly reminded him of that, but she was too proud to let herself sound that pathetic. At least to him…

She'd already admitted as much to his mother. But that had been in a weak moment. And she trusted Lilly Colton. In her, she'd found a kindred spirit more so than she had in her mother. But in raising this child alone, she was going to be more like her mother now—in the one way she'd vowed to never become her. But her mother had had no choice about being a single parent. Elise was choosing this over being with someone who didn't love her.

"And I told you that I would always love you," Neil insisted.

A cry burned the back of her throat, but she forced it out as a laugh. "You always divorce the people you love?"

"You know why I asked for the divorce."

"Asked?" She laughed again. If he'd asked, she would have told him no, just like she'd told him no to starting a family at that time.

But he'd replied that no time would ever be good for her. And maybe he'd been right. Because now, with someone trying to kill them, was not a good time.

"You know I didn't want to become my parents," he said, his brow furrowing.

"We'd be even more like them if we got married now," she said. "We'd be sticking together just for the sake of the kid—which is probably the same thing they've done, sticking together for the sake of all of you."

Neil sighed and pushed one of his hands through his thick, short hair. "Well, we're all grown up now, and they're still together."

She shrugged. "I can't explain your parents' marriage." Any more than she could explain hers. "I just know that I don't want it. Not for me. Not for you and especially not for this baby."

Neil's broad shoulders slumped as if he'd finally accepted defeat. And maybe he had because he nodded. Then he helped her set the table—well, the granite island—with plates and silverware. They ate together as they had so many times before, except that he hadn't cooked it and she hadn't picked up takeout.

"This is good," he said as he cleaned off his plate and reached for seconds.

She laughed. "You don't have to sound so damn surprised. See, our kid won't starve." She patted her stomach. Maybe she was finally getting over the nausea because she didn't feel sick now. At least not physically.

Emotionally, she wasn't sure she would ever get over Neil. And now they would share a child…

Better that they share a child than an enemy, though. "You started on the files," she prodded him when he'd gone curiously silent. "Anybody stick out to you?"

He sighed. "Everybody who didn't get away with their crimes."

She chuckled. "So a lot of somebodies."

"You know a lot of clients weren't happy if the deal we got them involved serving any jail time," he said. "So I forwarded those names to Jordana to check out which ones might have been paroled recently."

"Hopefully, there won't be many of them," she said. And then this would be over soon. "Unfortunately, they aren't the only unhappy ones in our old cases."

His brow furrowed as he stared at her. "I know you weren't crazy about practicing criminal law."

She smiled at how foolish she'd once been. "When I chose criminal law, I believed I'd have all these innocent clients to represent."

Neil grimaced. "Didn't turn out that way."

"Nothing turned out like I thought it would back in law school," she ruefully admitted. Most especially them…

"I'm sorry," Neil murmured. "I know I disappointed you."

"We disappointed each other," she said. "But I actually wasn't talking about my being unhappy. I was talking about the victims' families."

Neil groaned. "A lot of them were unhappy. Some of the suspects' families, too. I might be giving Jordana a very long list."

"Let's clear away these dishes," she said, "and start going through those files."

Neil glanced wistfully at that bare tree. "You sure you don't want to take a moment and do some decorating?"

She wanted to—badly. She wanted to turn on the Christmas music and dance around that tree like they had their first Christmas together. She wanted Neil—the way she'd had him that night, wearing nothing but the glow of those twinkling lights, as they'd made love over and over again.

If only they'd been able to restrict their passion to lovemaking and not to arguing.

But she knew they were too much alike to ever cohabitate amicably, and she didn't want to raise a child in an atmosphere of constant arguments. That would be even worse than the silent indifference with which Neil's parents treated each other.

"We really need to get a complete list of potential suspects to Jordana," Elise said.

Neil nodded. "I know…"

Perhaps they had finally found the one thing they

could easily agree on: they needed to find out who the hell was trying to kill them.

Ty ached to see Ashley again, but he was still reluctant to leave, even after the police car showed up to take over protection duty. Nevertheless, that car with its lights and *Braxville PD* emblazoned on it was probably more protection than he was. Sitting there on the street, in front of his brother's house, it was a visible deterrent to whoever was after them.

Accepting that they would be safe, Ty drove away, but doubts niggled at him yet. Was he doing the right thing? Would his brother and Elise be safe?

Chapter 20

She was so damn sexy. Black-framed reading glasses had slid down her nose like that oversize sweater had slipped off one shoulder. While she'd been studying their old case files, he'd been studying her.

She wasn't very far along in her pregnancy, but she had that famous glow that pregnant women were rumored to get. She seemed to radiate energy and life and beauty. And just watching her stole his breath away.

She glanced up and caught him staring. She arched one dark blond brow above the black frames in a quizzical expression. "What?"

He had to clear his throat, clear the desire from it, before replying with a question of his own, "Do you ever miss it?"

Furrows formed in her forehead, beneath a golden tress of hair. "Miss what?"

Them. He missed her so damn much, missed working with her, being with her...

"Our practice," he said.

"I told you that criminal law was not what I thought it was going to be," she reminded him. Then she sighed. "And it was never our practice. It was always yours." She glanced around the dark-paneled office. "Everything always felt like it was more yours than mine. This town. This house. Your family..." She shrugged. "I never really belonged."

Her admission stunned him. "You regret moving here with me after we graduated law school?"

She shook her head. "I didn't want to go back to Detroit. And I didn't want to stay in Boston." She shrugged. "But I just now feel like I've made my own life here."

Was that why she kept refusing his proposals?

"I would say that the town is more yours than mine now, Madam Mayor," he said. "Especially with how my family is being perceived."

She reached out then and ran her fingertips along his cheek. "Don't let Jeremy get to you."

He'd forgotten about his skirmish with her deputy mayor until she touched the slightly swollen area on his cheek. But it didn't hurt. It tingled instead from her touch. "Jeremy isn't the only one who's wondering what my father knew about his partner and why so many of the construction company employees have gotten sick."

Elise's fingertips slid along his cheek to the short

beard on his jaw. He kept it for her, because she'd always loved running her fingers over it. "I'm sorry," she murmured.

"Me, too," he said. "I just hope my dad…" He shook his head, unable to even put into words his fears for his father.

"I know," she said.

And she did.

Despite her own tense relationship with his father, she'd always been supportive of his.

Her fingers slipped away from his face, and she leaned back in the chair behind his desk, putting some distance between them. He sat in a chair on the side of it, close but not close enough.

He sighed, trying to shake off the tension inside him. But that tension wasn't just from his fears about his family or his and Elise's safety.

He was tense with desire for her. He wanted her so badly that his body ached. Though tempted, he didn't reach for her but instead for the legal pad on the desktop. They'd taken turns scribbling down names from the files—clients who'd wanted lighter sentences in the deals they'd negotiated. Victims' families who'd expressed outrage because they'd considered those sentences much too light.

"This is a long list," he said. "I should get it to Jordana so she and Reese can start working on it—see who's been released, where some of these people might have been last night and the night of the explosion."

She nodded. "Good idea."

He called his sister and read off the names to her.

"Wow," Jordana replied. "And I thought I had a lot of enemies."

"We might be overreacting," Neil admitted. "But we didn't want to miss anyone, which is why I think you should add Elise's deputy mayor to the list."

"Neil!" Elise exclaimed.

Jordana chuckled. "Just because you don't like him?"

"Let's say he has an unhealthy obsession with Elise."

Jordana chuckled again. "I would say he's not the only one."

He couldn't deny it. He'd been obsessed with his ex-wife since the moment he'd caught her looking at him in that law school lecture hall. She was so beautiful, so smart, so damn independent.

He'd never met anyone who challenged, infuriated or intrigued him as much as Elise did. And he had a feeling that he never would.

"Let's decorate the tree," Elise suggested. To get them out of the office. To get Neil's mind off his family drama. And her mind off him and how badly she wanted to kiss him.

When she'd run her fingertips along his beard, she'd wanted to lean closer, to brush her mouth over his. But she'd controlled the urge, not wanting to lead him on or to make him think that she might accept his proposal.

She also hadn't wanted to lead herself on...to believing that he might still love her. If he ever really had.

Maybe she had been as delusional about his feelings for her as she'd been about practicing criminal law. But she wasn't the naive girl she'd once been, not anymore. She jumped up from the chair behind the desk and headed out of the office, which was just off the foyer.

She glanced out the glass of the front door and breathed a sigh of relief at the sight of a police vehicle parked at the curb. They were safe here.

And maybe Jordana would be able to quickly figure out which of the many suspects on their list was responsible for the attempts on their lives. Then Elise would be able to return to her life.

For now she returned to the great room and stared up at the tree that Neil and his brother had set up near the fireplace. He took a little longer to join her, his arms full of the large plastic bins he must have brought out of the storage closet near the garage.

"Are you sure you want to decorate?" Neil asked her as he dropped the bins near the tree. "You're not still feeling all bah humbug?"

"Oh, I am," she said as she pulled a cover off the bin on top of the pile. She lifted out a silver ornament and studied it before putting it back inside the plastic tote. "I just don't want to think about that list you gave your sister."

"Jeremy?"

She shook her head. "Jeremy wouldn't hurt me…" She wished she could say the same for Neil. But she couldn't, and that was why she couldn't trust him with her heart again.

Neil touched his cheek, which she'd touched just a few minutes earlier. "He had no problem hurting me," he said.

"Poor baby," she teased him.

"You never offered to kiss it and make it better," he said. "That's what mothers are supposed to do."

"I'm not your mother," she said.

"No, you're not," he said. "But your kisses have always made everything better." His blue eyes twinkled with amusement as he flirted with her.

"Neil…" Temptation tugged at her, making her pulse quicken. Flirting with him was exciting, too exciting for her resist. So she stepped closer to him, rose on tiptoe and brushed her lips across his cheek.

But he quickly turned his head, and his mouth covered hers as he kissed her. Really kissed her.

Now her pulse raced as passion overwhelmed her. Why was she so weak when it came to Neil? She wanted to blame the pregnancy hormones, but if she hadn't been so irresistibly drawn to him, she wouldn't have been pregnant in the first place.

She slid her arms around his neck, clinging to him as his lips nibbled at hers. His tongue swiped across her bottom one, and she opened her mouth. He deepened the kiss, stealing her breath away as her heart hammered with desire.

He was such a good kisser. Always had been.

But then Neil was good at everything he did. Always had been…

Except marriage. Neither of them had been very good at it. They had been good at making love, though.

Wanting him too much to push him away, Elise clutched him closer and kissed him as deeply as he kissed her, tangling her tongue with his, nibbling at his lips.

He groaned and pulled back. "I don't want to stop. Do you?"

She shook her head. "No, I want you." So damn much…

His brow furrowed for a moment and he murmured, "I wish…" But then he shook off whatever maudlin thought had crossed his mind and swung her up in his arms.

She giggled and clutched his shoulders. "Hey, I'm getting too heavy for you to carry me."

"You're not even showing yet," he said. "You're light as a feather."

She laughed at his lie. She was curvy and soft, but she was happy with herself. And Neil had never seemed to have any complaints about her body.

After carrying her into the master bedroom, he quickly undressed her, pulling her sweater over her head and pushing down her leggings. When she stood before him wearing only thin bits of lace and satin, his breath escaped in a gasp. "You're so beautiful."

He'd always made her feel that way. A smile tugged at her lips, and she reached behind herself to unclasp her bra and let it drop to the floor.

He groaned.

Then she pushed down her panties. And he groaned again, more deeply.

"You're killing me," he said.

She flinched, momentarily reminded that someone was trying to do just that. Kill Neil…

And her…

She couldn't imagine a world without him in it. She

couldn't imagine being without him. So she reached out now, pulling at his zippers and buttons until he stood before her naked. He was perfect—in every way. All toned muscles, soft hair and sleek skin.

Her body throbbed with desire. She reached for him, but he stepped back and shook his head.

"I want you too much," he said. "If you touch me…"

She understood; that was how she wanted him—too much. Too much for her to have any control. Any resistance, any common sense…or she wouldn't be here, with him.

"I want to please you first," he said. He kissed her again, just lightly brushing his lips across hers before lowering his head. He kissed her neck, which always made her crazy with passion.

She clutched at his shoulders, trying to pull him closer. "You're pleasing me," she moaned.

Then he moved his head lower, to her breasts. He touched the tip of his tongue to one of her nipples, and her legs nearly folded beneath her as she shuddered with pleasure.

"You've always been so responsive," he said.

But she was even more so now, to his touch, to just the sight of him.

She'd never wanted anyone the way she'd wanted Neil. But now it was more than want—it was need.

She needed him inside her, needed to feel them move as one. She stepped back, toward the bed, and dragged him down with her. His weight settled heavily on her for just a moment before he rolled to his side.

"We have to be careful," he said.

"I'm not going to break," she assured him.

"Of the baby…"

A pang of disappointment struck her. Of course because of the baby. The baby was all he truly cared about.

While she knew that in her heart and in her head, her body had other ideas—other needs. And Neil satisfied those needs as his hands and mouth touched her everywhere. He pleased her—over and over again.

She called out his name and shuddered with release. And finally he moved, flopping onto his back, and pulled her astride him. She guided his erection inside her before settling onto him. He filled her—as he always had, filling the emptiness inside her.

But she wasn't empty anymore. She had a life growing inside her. A life they'd made together.

Neil gripped her hips, and she flinched as he found the bruise. He gasped and jerked his hand away. "I'm sorry. So sorry."

She wasn't sure what he was apologizing for—not now, not when he felt so damn good inside her. She forgot about her hip, about his not loving her, and she focused only on the pleasure he gave her. Neil moved his hands from her hips to her breasts, cupping them in his hands. He slid his thumbs across her nipples, and she cried out as she came.

But she kept moving, kept going for more, and another, more intense orgasm overwhelmed her.

Neil tensed and growled before his body shuddered as he came, too. Then he melted into the mattress, as boneless as she felt as she collapsed onto his chest.

He closed his arms around her, holding her close.

She could feel his heart hammering beneath her cheek. Could hear him panting for breath.

Then she heard something else—the trill of the doorbell. "Ty told you no more deliveries," she reminded him.

"I'm not having anything delivered." He'd tensed again. "But I should see who it is."

Panic flashed through her, and she clung to him as he rolled her to her side. "Don't go."

He chuckled. "I would love nothing more than to stay in this bed with you, but it could be Jordana. Maybe she got a lead off that list of names I gave her."

"That fast?" Elise asked doubtfully. "She's good but she's not that good."

He chuckled. "I won't tell her you said that."

Regretfully Elise watched as he covered up his gorgeous body, pulling on his jeans and sweater. But regret wasn't the only feeling plaguing her. She reached out and grasped his hand. "Don't go…"

The doorbell buzzed again. Whoever was waiting was getting impatient.

"Jordana knows the code," she said. "Your whole family does." She hadn't been happy when he'd given it to them after they'd first moved into their house. An only child, she hadn't been used to siblings just dropping by whenever they wanted to visit.

It wasn't a Colton ringing that bell.

So who was it?

"The killer isn't going to come up and ring the bell," Neil assured her.

But she wasn't as convinced. "I don't know."

* * *

The list of names that Neil had given her both overwhelmed and frightened Jordana. With her partner's help, she would whittle down the suspects. But in the meantime, she had to make sure that her brother and her ex-sister-in-law stayed safe.

She understood why Ty had needed a break, why he'd gone back to Wichita. Since Elise was the mayor, Braxville PD should be protecting her anyway. But still…

Jordana would have felt better if Ty had remained on the job. But Braxville PD had good officers.

She was good.

Still, she felt compelled to reach out to the officer posted outside Neil's house. First she tried the radio, but there was no response. Then she called dispatch, and the operator confirmed her fears. He hadn't checked in since arriving at the house.

Maybe he'd just fallen asleep. But her gut, and the instincts that had kept her alive while she'd been in the service, warned her that something else had happened to the officer.

Or somebody else had happened to him.

Had hurt him so that he hadn't been able to call out for help.

Chapter 21

Answer the damn door!

He probably didn't have much time before someone came to check on the officer. Or radioed him.

Even now, standing at the front door of Colton's custom-built house, he heard something from inside the patrol car. Was the officer waking up?

No. Not with as hard a blow as he'd got.

Maybe he would never wake up. That wouldn't be such a bad thing. In case he'd seen his face. Had he seen him? He'd been careful to lure him from his vehicle with the whole staged flat-tire drama. And he'd acted old and feeble so the officer stepped out to help him.

When the young man had gotten close enough, the tire iron had changed from a tool to a weapon and knocked him out. Blood spattered the pavement and the side of the rented vehicle. The tire was changed now. And so was the officer.

And so was he. He wore the young man's uniform… although it was a little tight, a little too tight. But Colton wouldn't have time to notice.

Because the tire iron had been replaced with the young officer's service revolver.

He had to get Colton to open the damn door, though. He had to get inside before he started firing so that neither of them had the chance to escape this time.

Impatience nagging at him, he pressed the bell again. Soon…

Soon he would get inside that damn house…and the lawyers would finally get what they deserved: death.

The doorbell buzzed again, making Neil wonder why his visitor was so damn impatient. Thinking maybe Elise was right to be concerned, he pulled out his cell phone. There was a camera at the front door, but before he opened the security app for the camera, he noticed a text from his sister.

Can't reach officer stationed at your house. I'm on my way. Don't do anything until I get there.

The text hadn't been sent long enough ago for his sister to be the one at the door. So Neil opened the security app. The man ringing the bell had his head down, face turned away, but his uniform was clearly visible, if a little ill fitting. The officer was at his door.

So why hadn't he checked in with Braxville PD?

As a criminal attorney, Neil knew all officers carried radioes on them, usually fastened to their shirt collars for easy communication. Most officers were equipped with body cams as well, which was partly the reason why Neil urged his clients to take plea deals instead of risking trials.

The uneasiness that Elise must have felt crept over Neil now, raising the short hairs on the nape of his neck. Something was off.

Could the officer be the one after them? Maybe he and Elise had gotten too good a deal for someone the cop had arrested.

They hadn't included the arresting officers of their clients on that list they'd given his sister.

Elise must have dressed quickly, because she caught up with him before he made it to the hall. She clutched his arm with one hand and her phone with the other. "Don't open the door!" she said. "Jordana sent a message."

His sister had apparently texted them both. Maybe because she hadn't trusted him to do nothing while he waited for her.

"I know," Neil said. "But it's the officer at the door." He showed the image on his phone to Elise.

Her brow furrowed as she studied his screen. "I don't know…"

"It is the officer," he insisted. "That's a Braxville PD uniform."

"Then why hasn't he answered your sister's calls?" Elise asked. "Just wait for her."

But the doorbell rang again. How many more times would the person ring before just forcing his way inside? The security system was good, but it wasn't foolproof.

As they watched the cell phone screen, the officer pulled out his weapon and pointed it toward the door. If he shattered the glass, he would be able to reach inside and turn the dead bolt. He and his gun would be able to get to them. And while the alarm would go off, police would not arrive immediately.

Maybe not in time to save them…

"I have a gun," Neil said. "It's in the safe, in the den."

Elise shook her head. "That's too close to the front door. If that isn't really an officer and he starts shooting through the glass…"

But Neil had to do something. He couldn't just cower inside his house while he waited for help to arrive. He had to make sure that his wife—*ex-wife*—and their unborn baby stayed safe.

"I bet it's the officer," Neil said, but it wasn't a bet of which he was sure enough to wager their lives. "I'll be perfectly safe. But just in case…"

"What?"

"Go to the garage, get in the SUV, and if you hear anything, get the hell out of here."

She shook her head. "No. I am not leaving you alone in here. Come with me. Leave with me."

But then the person would hear the garage door open and would be waiting for them.

Neil had to distract him. So, as he watched that

screen and saw the man's finger move along the barrel of his gun, he called out, "I'm coming!"

"You can't!" she exclaimed. "You have to wait for Jordana. She should be here soon."

Not soon enough. Not with the person already at his door pointing the gun at the glass...

If it was truly just the Braxville officer in a too-tight uniform, why would he have his weapon drawn and pointing at the house he was supposed to be protecting?

Neil sighed and shook his head as realization dawned. "He probably thinks something's happened to us because we haven't answered the door yet. We're just being paranoid."

"Cautious," Elise said. "We're being cautious."

Neil wanted to err on the side of caution, as well. "So go, get in the SUV."

"I don't have my purse or keys," she said. "They're upstairs."

"Mine are in the console of the vehicle, it's unlocked. Get in it and start it up," he advised her. Getting impatient himself, he gently shoved her toward the kitchen from which led the hall toward the service door of the garage. "Go!"

"Neil—"

"Go!"

He expected her to keep arguing, but instead she headed toward that door. Then he realized what she was doing—she was going to try to distract their visitor from the front door...just as he'd wanted to distract the person from her. "Damn it!" he called out.

She was going to get herself killed.

* * *

He was going to get himself killed—if she didn't act fast. Her heart pounding with fear for the man she loved, Elise ran to the garage and hit the switch for the garage door. The sound of it opening would distract their visitor from the front door.

But she hadn't realized that it would attract him to the garage before she even had a chance to jump in the SUV and start the engine. Within seconds of the garage door rising up to the ceiling, she had confirmation that they weren't just being paranoid about the officer.

And that he wasn't an officer...

Because shots rang out.

Like when the headlights had blinded her, she momentarily froze before she could even pull open the driver's door. She would have gotten hit for certain if something—or somebody—hadn't pushed her forward in front of Neil's vehicle and then knocked her to the ground. She recognized the shape and hardness of Neil's body as he covered hers with his.

She felt his heart pounding fast and heavily against her back, his breath panting in her ear. He was as scared as she was.

She had tried to stop him from putting himself in danger, but her misguided effort had put him in more peril. Glass from the SUV rained down on them, falling in her hair that was spread around her head.

Neil's hands covered her face to protect her from the glass, so she couldn't see much even though she turned her head. And she couldn't hear much, her ears ringing from the gunshot blasts.

Then silence fell. Neil's hands moved slightly. She could see more now—of the concrete floor and the undercarriage of Neil's vehicle and the black shoes on the other side of it.

But those shoes moved, as the shooter headed closer to them.

There was no way they would be able to avoid getting shot. In trying to save Neil, Elise was going to get him and herself killed.

Chapter 22

If only he'd retrieved his gun from his safe…

But there hadn't been time. If he hadn't acted when he had, Elise would already be dead. He wouldn't be able to protect her when he was dead, which probably could happen soon.

The gunfire stopped, but he heard the scrape of shoes against concrete as the shooter walked around the back of the SUV. Neil pulled Elise up, just enough to scoot her forward around the front of his SUV to the passenger's side. She must have been hit because he felt something wet against his hand. He'd tried to save her from getting hurt, but he must have been too late. She was alive, though, her body trembling against his.

He crouched low, keeping beneath the already shattered windows. And held his breath…

Then he heard the sirens. They wailed loudly as emergency vehicles approached. Those black shoes moved quickly now, running out of the garage and away from the house.

Neil released the breath he'd been holding. "Are you okay?" he asked Elise.

"I don't know."

"Did you get hit?" he asked as he stepped back and looked at her face. It was pale with fear except for a slight scrape on one cheek. He had done that, when he'd knocked her to the ground.

Her clothes were wrinkled, too, but that might have been from when he'd pulled them off earlier. He couldn't see any blood on her. So maybe that wetness he'd felt earlier had been tears.

Her eyes were dry now, though, and wide. "Is he gone?" she asked in a nervous whisper.

"I think so."

He raised his head to try to see which direction the man had gone. He couldn't get away—not again. He had to be stopped.

"Stay here," he told Elise as he leaned her against the passenger's side of the SUV. But before he could take more than a few steps, Elise grasped his arm and he flinched with pain.

"You're bleeding!" she exclaimed and jerked her hand from his wound.

He glanced down at his forearm, where blood saturated the torn sleeve of his sweater and trailed down his hand. "It doesn't hurt," he said.

But letting their assailant go, that would hurt.

"I'm fine," he insisted, and once free of her grasp, hurried out of the garage. The patrol car was still parked at the curb. The pseudo officer hadn't taken it.

So what had happened to the real officer?

Dread gripping his stomach, Neil started toward the cruiser. Before he could approach it, another police vehicle, lights flashing, pulled up next to it. It wasn't marked as clearly as the cruiser. But for the light on the dash and the government license plate, it might not have been real—just like the officer hadn't been real.

His sister jumped out of the passenger's side of this one, and there was no way anyone could impersonate Jordana, not even his other sisters. She was one of a kind and as tough as they came—until she saw that he was bleeding.

"Neil!" she yelled his name, her voice cracking with emotion. "Oh my God, are you okay?"

"No," Elise answered for him. "He's been shot."

Neil shook his head. "No, it's just a scratch." But he couldn't be certain what had scratched him. A bullet or some of the broken glass.

"What the hell happened?" Reese Carpenter asked the question as he jumped out of the driver's side. "We were coming over here to check on you and got the report of shots fired." He glanced into the garage and whistled. "Looks like the vehicle got the worst of it."

"I warned you to sit tight until we got here," Jordana said. "You have to stop putting yourself in danger and let me handle this."

"It was your officer at the door," Neil said. "With his gun drawn."

Jordana glanced toward the patrol car and shook her head. "No…" She pointed at Reese, who drew his weapon like she drew hers and they approached the parked vehicle. Once she got close enough to look inside, she cursed. "We need an ambulance," she called out before she even opened the back door. When she did, she reached inside and leaned over a limp body.

"Is he okay?" Neil asked with alarm.

"Unconscious," Jordana replied.

"But breathing," Reese added with an audible sigh of relief.

"Thank God," Neil murmured.

The police officer wasn't dead, and hopefully he wasn't hurt too badly. A pang of guilt struck him that the man had been hurt protecting them, though. Compounding the guilt was relief that it hadn't been Ty who'd been hurt. But maybe his brother would have caught whoever had knocked out the officer.

Jordana must have been thinking the same thing because she murmured, "Too bad Ty left."

"We don't know that he would have been able to protect us," Neil said. He might have gotten hurt worse than the officer was. Neil wasn't sure that anyone would be able to protect them.

Elise couldn't stop shaking. Why the hell had she been so stupid? She could have gotten herself and Neil killed. She wasn't any more rational than he was. Which made it just too damn dangerous for them to stay together.

"You need to go to the hospital," she said when the ambulance arrived.

He shook his head. "The officer is hurt far worse than I am."

The young man had regained consciousness, but it was clear that he was in pain. Neil was, too, wincing every time he brushed his bleeding arm against something.

"Your wound hasn't stopped bleeding," she said, pointing out the small pool of blood forming on the driveway beneath his hand that dangled at his side. "You have to get stitches."

"She's right," Jordana agreed, but the ambulance was already speeding away, lights and sirens going, behind a police escort.

"Was he able to tell you anything?" Neil asked his sister, pointing toward the departing ambulance.

She sighed. "He got conned. Guy pulled up on the street with a flat tire, acted like he was struggling with it. When Officer Lester walked over to help, the man hit him with the tire iron, knocking him out."

"Was the officer able to give you a description?" Neil asked.

She shook her head. "Sunglasses and hat pulled so low that he couldn't say what color his hair or eyes were. And with him crouching next to the car, he couldn't even tell how tall he was."

"What about the car? Was he able to describe it?"

Jordana shrugged. "What does it matter? I doubt it belonged to him. He probably stole that one, too. What can you two tell me about the guy? What did you see?"

Anger gripped Elise, anger at the lunatic who'd tried to kill them and anger at herself for putting them in danger. "I didn't see anything," she said. "But his damn shoes..."

"I showed you my phone with the video from the security camera at the front door," Neil reminded her.

She shook her head. "I didn't have my glasses on."

"What did you see on that video?" Jordana asked her brother.

Neil shook his head. "Not much," he admitted. "He kept his face turned away from the front door."

"So he either knew about the security camera or he didn't want you to recognize him before you'd opened the door," Jordana surmised.

"So we might know who he is," Elise said. "He's not just some hired hitman, then."

"If he was a professional, you would probably already be dead," Jordana said.

And Elise couldn't argue that; they'd had too many close calls.

"Did you notice anything else about him?" the detective asked.

"The uniform was too tight on him," Neil said.

"So he's bigger than Officer Lester," Jordana said.

"I wish I could tell you more," Neil said with a groan over his frustration. Then he raised his arm, probably to push his hand through, his hair, and a grimace of pain contorted his handsome face.

Concern grasped Elise's heart. "You need a doctor to look at that wound."

"Yes, I'll take you to the hospital," Jordana said.

"And you can send Yvette the video. Maybe she can use her crime tech skills to find something else that might help us identify this guy."

Elise let out a soft sigh of relief that his sister was also pushing him to seek treatment. And while he was gone, she intended to pack up her stuff and head some-where—anywhere—else. It was too dangerous for them to be together.

It was too much temptation for their assailant to try to take them both out at the same time. And it was too much temptation for Elise to fall into Neil's bed and back in love with him.

Yvette rewound the footage and watched it again, watching as the man pulled the gun and pointed it to-ward the glass in Neil's front door. Despite the uniform he wore, he wasn't there to check on Yvette's brother and the mayor. He was there to kill them.

"Come on, come on," she murmured. "Turn toward the camera. Look at me…"

But he kept his face turned away from the front door, showing only his profile. Who the hell was he?

She rewound again…to when he started walking up toward the house. Something about his walk…

It was vaguely familiar.

Uncle Shep…

A smile curved her lips as she thought of her favorite family member. Of course, it wasn't him in that uniform with the gun. But the way this man carried himself re-minded her of her dad's brother.

"You look pleased with yourself," Jordana remarked

as she joined her in the tech lab. "You found something?"

Yvette pointed at the screen. "Who does that walk remind you of?"

"Military bearing," Jordana remarked.

Of course she would recognize it. Like Uncle Shep, she had served, too.

"I'll ask Neil which of his former clients might have been in the military," Jordana said.

"Is he okay?" Yvette asked, concern for her brother gripping her. Ty had been shot last month, and now someone was trying to kill Neil.

"Physically, yes," Jordana said. "He just needed a few stitches for a cut on his arm."

"Emotionally, I can understand why he'd be upset," Yvette said. "Someone's trying to kill him."

"He's pissed about that," Jordana said. "But I'm more worried how he's going to react to finding out Elise is gone."

Yvette gasped with horror. "What? The killer got to her? She's dead?"

"Not dead," Jordana quickly assured her. "She just doesn't want to stay with Neil anymore."

"I'm surprised she agreed to stay with him at all," Yvette said.

"They still love each other," Jordana said.

"Then why won't she stay with him?" Yvette asked.

She did not understand why people in love acted so damn crazy. She wanted no part of that; she wanted only to focus on her work. She could make a difference with it—do some good now.

"I suspect that's why she won't stay with him," Jordana said. "She also thinks they'll be safer if they're not together. She's probably right. But Neil won't see it that way…"

"And it doesn't mean that their assailant won't still get to both of them…"

The man had been bold enough to take down a cop and risk getting caught on the security video. He wasn't going to give up.

Chapter 23

She was gone.

Neil knew it the minute he walked in the door. When she'd refused to go to the hospital with him, he'd realized she was planning to pack up and leave him.

Just like she had three years ago.

That time it had been his fault. His impatience spurring him on to give her an ultimatum. He should have been more patient this time. He should have stopped pressuring her to accept his proposal.

He reached for his phone to call her, to beg her to come back, but then he noticed the text she had sent him.

We're safer apart than together.

She was probably right. But he didn't care if his life was in more danger when he was with her. He cared only about keeping her and their unborn baby safe.

The cell vibrated, startling him. Jordana.

"Did you find something?" he asked anxiously. They had to catch this person.

"We think the guy might have a military background," she said.

"Because of the bomb?"

"Possibly," she said. "But even just the way he walked up to the door."

Neil hadn't seen that part of the video. He'd been preoccupied—with Elise. He couldn't imagine sleeping in that bed now without her. He didn't know how he'd managed to get used to sleeping alone the past few years, but he didn't want to get used to it again.

"He reminded Yvette of Uncle Shep," Jordana continued, her voice warming as she spoke of their uncle.

While the career Navy man hadn't been around much when they were growing up, he had made an impact on all of their lives. He was such a good man. An honorable man.

Neil wished he could say the same, with all confidence, of his father. But he just wasn't sure anymore…

"I'll look through the case files again," Neil told his sister.

"Not tonight," Jordana said.

"She wants to go home to Clint and not be interrupted," Yvette called out from the background of wherever his sisters were.

Jordana continued as if her little sister hadn't interrupted her, "Get some rest. It's late. Let me know tomorrow if you remember any clients with a military background."

Clients…

Maybe he'd had a couple of them, men who'd struggled after returning from combat. But he didn't remember any of them threatening him or Elise. Something else flitted through his mind, though.

He'll get what's coming to him.

"Did you already fall asleep?" Jordana asked.

"No." He doubted he was going to be able to sleep at all.

"You're safe, you know," she said.

"It's not me I'm worried about," he admitted.

"I know. There's a patrol car parked outside both your homes," she said. "And after what happened to Officer Lester, they're going to be extra vigilant. Braxville PD wants this guy as much as you do."

"Officer Lester is going to be okay," he reminded her. The other Braxville PD personnel gathered in the waiting room had confirmed that their comrade had a concussion but was expected to recover.

"I know," Jordana said. "It's just that we now know exactly how dangerous this guy is."

"I already knew that," Neil said, letting the irony slip into his voice. But he had learned something new and not just about the guy's military background; he'd learned exactly how determined the man was to kill him and Elise.

So determined that he wasn't likely to give up until he'd been caught or until he was dead.

"Be careful," Jordana told him. Needlessly.

The minute their call ended, Neil headed into the den. He opened the safe in the wall behind his desk and pulled out the gun he should have had on him earlier. Maybe then this would have been over already.

He had the gun for protection.

What did Elise have...besides that patrol car?

Elise was tired and not just from her recent sleepless nights, not even from growing the baby inside her. She was exhausted from clearing away enough of the destruction in her condo so that she could sleep. While she was no neat freak, the chaos was unsettling. But the chaos wasn't just inside her condo; it was inside her heart and her head, as well.

She'd wanted to go to the hospital with Neil, like he'd beseeched her. She'd wanted to hold his hand while he got the stitches he'd obviously needed to stop the bleeding. She'd wanted to return to their home with him and to their bed and to pretend they'd never gotten divorced.

That it had all been a bad dream.

But that wasn't possible. Elise was too much of a realist, and she knew that reality would come crashing down around her if they tried to make a go of it just for the baby's sake.

Her cell phone, sitting on the nightstand next to her bed, vibrated. Already knowing who it was, she reached for it, accepted the call and said, "I'm not coming back to your house. This is for the best."

"It's not," Neil said. "You know what would be best. For all of us."

"Neil…"

"But I'm not going to pressure you," he said. "I just want to make sure you're safe."

"There's a police car parked in my driveway," she assured him. And if she wanted, as mayor, she could use city funds to hire additional security. She just didn't want to do that, didn't want that to be necessary. She wanted their would-be killer caught soon.

"There's one here, too," he said.

She had no doubt that his sister would have made certain he was protected, just as she'd made certain he'd received stitches, too.

"Are you okay?" she asked.

"No."

"I thought it was just a cut," she said.

"It is just a cut," he said. "I was talking about your not being here with—"

"Stop," she interjected. "Or I'm going to hang up on you." That was what she should have done when he'd divorced her—stopped having any contact with him. But they had promised to be civil and to work together on the loose ends from their former business and personal relationships.

"I have another reason for calling," he said. "Jordana and Yvette think the person after us might be military."

"Because of the bomb? Can't anybody make one of those off YouTube videos nowadays?"

"I think it was more to do with the way he walked, according to them," he said. "And the bomb was more complicated than something someone without any experience could have made."

"Oh, then that makes sense," she murmured in agreement. "And that leaves out Jeremy."

Neil cursed as if he was really disappointed, but then he begrudgingly admitted, "I didn't think it was him on the security footage. Jeremy doesn't ever hide from cameras. He seeks them out."

She chuckled. She should have been happy to rule out her deputy mayor, but she found herself suggesting, "He could have hired someone to get rid of us."

"No, this feels too personal," Neil said.

"But then wouldn't we have figured out who it was by now?" she asked. Her head was beginning to pound with exhaustion and with frustration. How could they not have any idea who was after them?

"It's been a few years since we practiced together," he said. "It's understandable that while we might remember the clients, we could have forgotten other people associated with those cases. I keep thinking it might be a victim's family member."

Her skin chilled as she remembered someone shouting out in the courtroom after the judge had accepted their plea deal and sentence recommendation.

He'll get what's coming to him.

"There was someone," she murmured. "A dad or a brother of a woman who died."

"Dad," Neil said. "It was her dad. He wanted his daughter's husband sentenced to death, and instead he got a light sentence for manslaughter."

"Our client wasn't happy with the sentence, either," Elise remembered. "He kept claiming he was innocent." She'd hoped he was, but she hadn't been convinced, and neither would the jury have been. If she'd truly believed he was innocent, she would have told him to reject the plea. It had been more than fair…unless the murder had been premeditated, like the victim's family had believed.

"But we pointed out that the prosecution had enough evidence for a conviction," Neil said, "so he accepted the deal for manslaughter."

"Nobody was happy with that case," she agreed. Just thinking of it, of that poor woman's death, unsettled her. Had it been a heat-of-the-moment, almost-accidental death like Neil had convinced the prosecutor it must have been?

"I'll call Jordana back," he said, then chuckled.

"What?"

"I'm not supposed to disturb her tonight, though."

"Don't, then," she said. "It's late. Let her get some sleep."

"Will you?" he asked.

"I'm exhausted," she admitted.

"But will you be able to sleep?" he asked. "I won't. Not without you."

Temptation pulled at her. She would like nothing more than to lie in his arms, with her head on his chest, in the bed they'd once shared. But she couldn't trust him with her heart again. Not when it still hadn't healed from the last time he'd broken it and not when she knew he only wanted to be with her again because she was pregnant. If she'd lost the baby that first night he'd found out, the night of the explosion, he never would have proposed in the first place.

Needing all of her energy to fight the temptation to go back to him, to that house, she didn't argue. She simply hung up her phone.

Damn it.

How could he have fired so many shots and missed them? Well, he'd missed her. Colton had gone to the hospital, but he'd been released—and driven home by a police officer.

Police officers were stationed at both their places now. He wouldn't be able to get to them like he needed to. He wouldn't be able to finish them first like he'd planned.

He would have to go on to his next target.

But he'd be back…

Eventually their security would slip up or they would, and he would end their miserable lives like he should have years ago.

Chapter 24

Neil studied the man as he walked toward them. He was tall and leanly muscled, with a certain bearing that commanded attention even across the crowded restaurant. "So that's the military walk?" he asked his sisters.

"Yup," Jordana confirmed and she jumped up to greet the man. Instead of saluting him, as Neil half expected she might, she hugged him.

Yvette hugged him next, and the man clasped her a little more tightly than he had Jordana. But that might have been just because she wasn't armed like their older sister. Once he released Yvette, he clasped Neil's proffered hand tightly.

"It's so good to have you home, Uncle Shep," Jordana said, gushing.

Uncle Shep pushed up the bill of his ball cap a little,

and his brown eyes warmed with affection. "Glad to be home." He looked at each of them for a long moment before narrowing his eyes slightly and asking, "Why do I think you didn't ask me to meet you here just for breakfast?"

La Dolce Vita probably hadn't been the smartest place to meet at all—not with how Megan Chase kept glaring at them. Her husband had worked for Colton Construction…before he'd gotten sick. So very sick.

Neil ignored the proprietress's scowl and focused on his uncle. "I need your help, Uncle Shep," he admitted.

Uncle Shep nodded. "I heard about somebody going after you and the mayor. I'm happy to help out anyway I can." He slid into the booth next to Yvette.

The three of them filled him in on everything that had happened and shared the security footage and information on the bomb with him.

"I'd say your assailant definitely has some military training," he agreed.

Yvette and Jordana nodded in agreement of his conclusion. Before they could say anymore, their cell phones rang. "We have to leave," Jordana said.

"Duty calls," Yvette agreed.

Neil's heart jumped in his chest. "Elise? Has something happened to Elise?"

"No, not at all," Jordana assured him. "Her protection detail assured me she is safe at City Hall as we speak."

"This has nothing to do with you," Yvette assured him. "I have a robbery scene to process."

"And for me to investigate," Jordana added with a smile.

After more hugs for Uncle Shep, they left. Neil reached for his cup of coffee, and his hand shook slightly in reaction to his fear that something might have happened to Elise.

"You're really worried," Uncle Shep remarked.

He nodded. "This guy just keeps coming for us."

"Any idea who?"

"We've narrowed it down to a former client and maybe his victim's family. When we first started our practice we represented a man, Seth Costner, accused of murdering his wife, Leah. He claims he didn't do it, but there were enough witnesses and circumstantial evidence for the DA to get a conviction. We got him a deal instead."

"Didn't he think it was a deal?" Uncle Shep asked.

Neil shook his head. "He swears he was innocent."

"You didn't believe him?"

Neil shrugged. "I don't know. His wife's family sure didn't, and they thought he should have gotten the death penalty. Her dad, Walter Shultz, yelled out in court that he was going to get what's coming to him."

"Has he?" Shep asked.

"We're checking to see if he's been paroled."

"He might be in danger if he has," Shep said. "Or he might be who's coming after you."

"I don't think Seth had any military training, though."

"Let me check," Shep murmured as he pulled out his cell phone. He didn't make his call in the diner, though. He stepped outside instead.

No longer hungry or thirsty, Neil dropped some

money on the table to pay his and his sisters' bill and joined his uncle outside, where a patrol car was parked at the curb. His security detail.

With his uncle present, he doubted he needed additional backup. Despite his recent retirement from the Navy, Shep was in great shape and maybe not so retired that he didn't still have connections.

Neil couldn't overhear much of the conversation, with his uncle keeping his voice to a gruff whisper. But it wasn't long before Shep disconnected the call and said, "I don't think Seth Costner is your man."

"Damn," Neil said. "I thought it was a good lead."

"It is," Shep replied. "Because I think it's Costner's former father-in-law who's going after you. Walter Shultz has the military experience with explosives, and as an excavator he still has access to explosives."

"So he could be making more damn bombs as we speak," Neil murmured. More bombs that he could be planting to kill him and Elise.

He needed to check on her—personally—to make sure she really was safe. But first he had to know, "How did you find all that out so quickly?"

Uncle Shep flashed his quick grin. "I have my ways."

"I thought you retired your ways," Neil said.

The grin turned slightly sheepish. "I still have connections. And I have some experience investigating."

"In the Navy?"

"Navy Intelligence," Shep admitted.

"Oh…" That made so much sense now. "Jordana takes after you so much."

"Yvette, too," Shep said. "With the investigating…"

Neil nodded. "Hopefully they can use those skills to track down Walter Shultz." Before he built another bomb. Before he tried to hurt him or Elise again.

"They will," Shep assured him. "You need to let them do their jobs."

Neil groaned. "Please don't tell me to stay out of it. I can't—not when there are so many lives in danger. Mine, Elise's and our…"

Shep tilted his head and peered at Neil. "Your what?" he asked.

Neil hadn't shared their news with any of their family. And his mother wouldn't have, either, since she was fanatical about those privacy laws. He could have told his family, but he'd wanted to wait…until Elise had agreed to marry him again. He doubted that was ever going to happen, though.

So he told his uncle, "Our unborn baby's."

"Elise is pregnant?" Shep asked, his brown eyes wide with surprise.

Neil nodded. "Yes, and it's mine." In case his uncle wondered.

Shep chuckled. "Of course it is. You two might be divorced, but I don't think there will ever be anyone else for either of you."

"Not for me," Neil confirmed. "But Elise refuses to give me another chance." He'd screwed up too damn badly when he'd asked for the divorce.

Uncle Shep squeezed his shoulder. "Don't give up. A love like that…" he cleared his throat "…like yours is worth fighting for. Don't give up, Neil, or you'll spend the rest of your life regretting it."

He'd already spent the past three years regretting the divorce.

"And be careful," Uncle Shep cautioned, "so that you have a long life to spend with the woman you love and the child you've created."

Emotion choked Neil at his uncle's words, and he could only nod in agreement. His uncle had always been a confirmed bachelor, but now it sounded like that hadn't been his choice. And that he regretted not fighting for the woman he'd loved.

Neil had already spent too much time dwelling on regrets. He was going to make sure that he didn't have cause for any more.

He hadn't been lying. With the dark circles beneath his eyes and his mussed hair, Neil looked as if he hadn't slept at all last night. But Elise doubted that it was for the reason he'd claimed on the phone the previous evening— because she hadn't been in his arms, in his bed. There was no place she would have rather been...if he loved her.

If only he loved her...

He hadn't even spoken to her yet. Since walking into her office, he'd been on his cell with one of his sisters. He paced the small confines of her office, his handsome face tense as he listened.

Exhausted just from watching him, she leaned back in her chair. She already knew what he must have learned. The minute he disconnected his call, she said, "Seth Costner was paroled last week."

He nodded. "Even earlier than the deal we made for him."

"Good behavior is the reason his parole officer gave me," she said. "He also said that he's still proclaiming his innocence."

Neil sighed. "I don't know what to believe about that, but it's clear that his father-in-law holds him responsible for his daughter's murder."

"Manslaughter," Elise murmured. An accident. That was what Seth had claimed it was. His father-in-law had insisted it had been planned, that the couple had been fighting nonstop. "And how is it clear that his father-in-law still holds him responsible? Has he gone after him?"

"I don't know about Seth, but I think Walter Shultz is who's gone after us. Uncle Shep confirmed he's former military, with experience in explosives and current access to them."

She was glad she was sitting down, since her legs started shaking. "That's why you told Carmen not to allow any packages up here." When she'd overheard him talking to her assistant, she'd figured he was worried about explosives.

He nodded. "We have to be extra careful until this guy is caught."

Even after he was caught, she had to be extra careful so she didn't fall back in love with her ex-husband. "Are Jordana and Reese looking for him?"

He nodded. "But they haven't tracked him down yet. They're looking for Seth, too. Does his parole officer know where he is?"

She glanced down at the paper on her desk, at the address his parole officer had given her. She'd intended to call Jordana and give her the information. But she hadn't had a chance before Neil entered.

He stepped closer to her desk and picked up the slip of paper. "Is this it?" he asked.

"You need to give that to your sister," she said. "That's what I was going to do."

"It's more important that she focus on finding Shultz," Neil said. "I can stop by Seth's and warn him that his ex-father-in-law might be gunning for him like he's been gunning for us."

Her legs were shaking even more now, but she jumped up from her chair anyway. "No!" she exclaimed. "You need to stay away from him."

"It's not him," Neil insisted. "It's Shultz."

"And Shultz could be going after him right now," she said. "And you could walk right into the middle of a bad situation if you go see him."

"He needs to be warned," Neil insisted.

"I'll call his parole officer back," she said. "I'll have him warn him."

"Seth might also have some idea where Shultz could be," Neil said. "I need to talk to him myself."

"No, you don't need to—you want to," she said. "You want to put yourself in danger."

"I want to put an end to the danger," he insisted. "I want to make sure you're safe."

"Me? Or the baby?" she asked.

His brow furrowed. "What do you mean? Both of you, of course."

If only she could be certain of that.

"All of us," he said. "Seth, too."

"That's not your job," she said. "Leave that to the police to handle."

"What if we were wrong?" he asked. "What if he was innocent?"

"Then he'd be as mad at us as Walter Shultz is," she said. And she wouldn't blame him. "But he didn't have to take the deal. He could have taken his chances with a trial."

Neil nodded. "He could have, but we strongly warned him against doing that. And I need to strongly warn him now about his father-in-law."

"He probably already knows," she said. It might have been too late for Seth. She didn't want it to be too late for Neil, too. "Don't go!" She grasped his arm, holding onto him so he wouldn't leave.

"I'm doing this for us," he insisted. "And to protect you."

"I don't need your protection," she replied. She needed his love. But she was too proud to admit it and too damn mad at him for not listening.

He groaned with frustration of his own. "I know you're fierce and independent and think you can take care of yourself. But it's not just you anymore. You're carrying my baby. And I will do whatever necessary to protect you both!" He pulled from her grasp and headed out of her office.

She could have chased him, but she knew he wasn't going to stop for her. He was too damn stubborn. So she went back to the pad on her desk, from which she'd torn off the first sheet of paper. She ran the edge of a pencil over the page and the address stood out in white.

Her hand shaking, she punched in Jordana's number.

"Elise, everything okay?" the detective asked.

"No," she replied and filled the young woman in on what her brother was doing.

Jordana cursed. "He has a car following him. I'll make sure they stick close and don't let him get in any trouble."

"What about you?" Elise asked. "Can you get to him before he makes it to that address?"

Jordana cursed again. "No. Reese and I are out of town—where we were told Walter Shultz was working. But he's not at the job site."

Which meant that he could be with Seth, which meant that Neil would be too late to save him. What about Neil? Would the officers following him be able to protect him?

Jordana wouldn't be able to make it any time soon to the address Elise had given her, but Elise might be able to—just probably not in time to save Neil if Shultz was there, though. But she couldn't wait in her office until she knew what had happened.

She had to go there, too, had to check on the man she loved, the father of her baby. If the police officers weren't able to protect him, what would she tell her child about his or her father?

That the man had given up his life to protect theirs...

Maybe he should have started here, with Seth. But his intention had been to frame the killer for the murders of his lawyers. Seth wouldn't have lived to accept another plea deal, though. Walter would have made cer-

tain of that. Seth would have had a horrible accident—
like the one he'd claimed Leah had had.

But her death had been no accident. It had been murder. Not manslaughter, like his slimy lawyers had convinced the prosecutor and the judge it was.

"I didn't do it, Walt," Seth whined from where he
lay on the scuffed hardwood floor.

Walter had knocked him down the minute Seth Costner had walked into the old Costner family cabin. He
hadn't known he was there because Walter had parked
his vehicle over a mile away. He could use Seth's to
leave here once he was done, once Seth was done. Blood
trickled from the corner of the weasel's thin lips, and
Walter's knuckles stung. So he kicked him instead, driving his steel-toed boots into his former son-in-law's ribs.

Seth cried out in pain. "Stop. Please stop."

Fury rushed through Walter, nearly blinding him. "Is
that what Leah did? Did she beg you to stop?"

"It wasn't like that, Walt," he insisted. "I didn't see
her in the garage. I accidentally ran her over…"

"Shut up!" Walt raged. "The coroner said her injuries were inconsistent with a vehicle—more like a fist.
You beat her to death just like I'm going to beat you
to death."

Seth whimpered and tried crawling across the floor.
He wasn't going to get far—at least not alive. And if
he tried to run…

Well, Walt still had the gun from the other night. And
this time he wasn't going to miss. But before he could
drag Seth back, a noise drew his attention to the win-

dow. The crunch of gravel as a car slowly approached the cabin.

Who the hell had chosen to visit an ex-con now? Then he recognized the man behind the wheel and grinned. At least one of the lawyers had showed up.

Chapter 25

Neil had lost the patrol car that had been following him. He'd done it inadvertently, though. Maybe—because there were so many white sedans like the one he'd rented—they'd lost him in traffic. He hadn't realized they weren't there until he'd turned onto the gravel road leading to the cabin that Seth Costner had listed with the parole office as his current address. Full of deep ruts, it appeared the road wasn't well maintained and probably not often traveled.

But then Seth had only been released the week before, so he'd not been staying at the cabin very long. He must have inherited the property when his parents died while he was in prison.

It was possible he still harbored resentment toward Neil for encouraging him to accept the plea deal. But

Neil was less concerned about Seth hurting him than he was about Walter Shultz hurting all of them.

Did Walter know where Seth was staying? Had he known about the cabin?

The house Seth had lived in with his wife, Leah, had belonged to his former father-in-law, just as Seth had also worked for the man. Walter Shultz had been a highly controlling man. He'd also been composed, but for that one outburst he'd made in the courtroom after sentencing.

He'd been furious about the manslaughter sentence. How must he have felt over Seth being released early due to good behavior? Maybe Seth was already dead.

As he turned onto the drive leading to the cabin, Neil noticed a plume of smoke rising above the trees, and when he drew closer, he saw it above the chimney sticking out of the roof the cabin. Someone had recently started the fire in the hearth, so Seth might still be here.

And with only one vehicle parked in the drive, it was probably just Seth.

Neil stopped his car behind Seth's battered pickup, which he'd probably inherited along with the cabin. Then he reached into the glove compartment for the gun he'd taken from his safe the night before. He wasn't taking the risk Elise thought he was.

He was prepared this time. Not that he wanted to use it, but thanks to his father and his uncle, he knew how to shoot. He even occasionally visited the shooting range with Jordana and Ty.

He had never pointed a weapon at a real person, though. Just a target. But if he had to use the gun, he would, because he wasn't just defending himself now; he was defending his family. The family he'd wanted for so long.

So why wouldn't Elise accept his proposal and make them a family again?

Suddenly, realization dawned on him like a slap upside the head. God, he wished now that she had slapped him—instead of getting that look on her face that she'd gotten every time he proposed or talked about the baby.

She thought that was all he wanted.

That all he cared about was the baby she carried...

His ears buzzed as he remembered his mother saying something like that to him, in the waiting room after the hit and run, but he'd been so worried about Elise that he hadn't fully understood what they'd both meant.

Elise didn't think he loved her. How the hell could she, after he'd divorced her just because she'd wanted to wait before having kids?

How could he have been so stupid?

Shaking his head in self-disgust, he stepped out of his car. At once, a gun barrel pressed to the back of his head, and he realized just how blind he'd been. He hadn't even noticed the man sneaking out of the house and up on his vehicle.

"Nice of you to join us, lawyer," Walter Shultz said.

"Us?" God, he hadn't somehow gotten to Elise and then beat him here, had he?

"I presume you've come by to talk to your client," Shultz said. "You better talk fast, because I'm not sure how much longer he's going to last."

Seth wasn't dead yet. But, apparently, he was dying.

And once he was dead, Neil had no doubt that he would be next. He couldn't die, though, not without making sure that Elise knew how much he loved her, how much he had always loved her.

"What do you mean you lost him?" Jordana exclaimed, her voice rattling her cell phone with the frustration and fear gripping her. "You're supposed to be sticking close to him. Too close to lose him."

Oh, God, Elise had been right; Neil was going to get himself killed.

"This is where he was headed," she said, reading off the address that Elise had given her. "And I hope like hell you're closer than we are."

Reese pressed harder on the accelerator as he steered around slower-moving vehicles. Hell, everything on the freeway was moving slower than they were as he raced past them, lights and sirens flashing. "You don't even know that Shultz is there," Reese said. "You might be worried about nothing."

Every instinct she possessed screamed out in protest. "It's not nothing. Shultz wasn't where he told his office manager he'd be. He has a reason for that, a reason for being somewhere else."

"With Seth Costner?" Reese asked. "With the man who murdered his daughter?"

"Exactly," she said.

Reese groaned. "You think he's killing him."

And she shared Elise's fear that her brother was walking blindly into the middle of that murder to his own. "I don't know if he would set up a bomb or just shoot him."

"Do we need to send out a bomb squad?" Reese asked. "A sniper?"

She would…if she thought any of them would arrive in time to save her brother. But she didn't even believe that she was going to arrive in time to save Neil.

Elise was a good driver, but she'd never taken a defensive driving class or participated in a car chase. So instead of driving herself to the address the parole officer had given her, she'd climbed into the back seat of the patrol car parked outside City Hall. And when the unit following Neil radioed in that they'd lost him, she was damn glad that she had her protection duty.

Not just for her protection but also so that they could maybe save Neil, as well. Of course he didn't believe that he was in serious danger from Seth Costner. He just wanted to warn the parolee that his father-in-law might want to kill him.

Elise was pretty sure that Seth was already aware of how Walter Shultz felt about him. What she hadn't realized was how the man might have felt about her and Neil.

Was he really the one who'd tried to kill them?

"Are you all right, Mayor Willis?" one of the officers asked her through the metal screen separating the front of the car from the back. Since the young officer had been hurt outside Neil's house, two officers were now assigned to each of them.

Two hadn't been enough for Neil, though, since he'd lost them. What the hell had he been thinking?

Of the baby, probably.

She slid her palm over her stomach, and something fluttered inside her. Maybe it was just nerves, but she wondered if it could be the baby moving restlessly, also worried about his father. Would they ever meet?

Even before getting pregnant, she'd worried about becoming a single parent like her mother. She'd feared that her baby might be abandoned like she had been. She shouldn't have suspected that Neil, who'd wanted a family of his own so badly, would ignore his child. But now she knew that while he might not do it willingly, he might still abandon him or her.

"Mayor?" the officer called out to her.

She was bouncing around on the back seat as the car traveled down a gravel road with deep ruts in it. Grasping the armrest, she assured the officer, "I'm fine."

"Is this it? The right address?" the driver asked, voice doubtful.

She glanced at the piece of paper with the numbers and letters standing out in relief against the gray pencil lead. "I—I think so."

She couldn't be entirely sure, though, that the four wasn't a nine or maybe a seven. Not that it could have made much difference. There weren't many houses out here. In fact all she'd seen was trees dusted with snow on either side of the road and now on either side of the driveway down which they traveled.

Finally a gap widened between the trees, revealing a

small cabin nearly obscured by the two vehicles parked in front of it. "There's someone here."

And from the sticker on the back bumper, it was clear one of the vehicles was a rental. Neil had had to rent one while his vehicle was being repaired from being shot up in the garage the night before.

"Yes," she said. "This has to be the right place." As the officers stepped out of the police cruiser, she reached for her door handle. But it didn't budge. She would have to wait for them to let her out.

But before they could, gunshots rang out.

Now she had no doubt: Neil was here. Or he had been...

Was he dead now?

Chapter 26

As the gun blasted, Neil flinched, bracing himself for the bullet to strike. The barrel had been pressed against his head for so long, but then the police car had pulled into the driveway. And Walter Shultz had reacted, turning his gun toward the window...toward Elise.

Because somehow Neil knew she was in that car, that she'd brought along her security detail to stop him from putting himself in danger. From impatiently rushing into a situation without thinking of the consequences.

He'd done that too many times. The worst time had been when he'd told Elise he'd wanted a divorce. He hadn't thought that through, hadn't imagined what it would be like to live without her.

And he didn't want to find out now, either. So when Walter turned that gun toward the window, Neil reacted. He jumped the former soldier and wrestled him for the weapon.

While Walter was older than him, like Uncle Shep, he was still in great shape. Strong and more than that, crazed with rage and determination.

He'd nearly killed his former son-in-law, or so Neil had thought when Walter had escorted him, with the gun barrel pressed to the back of his head, into the cabin. Seth had been lying on the floor, bleeding from his nose and mouth. Unconscious.

Or so Neil had believed.

But as he rolled around on the floor with Walter, struggling to hold the gun barrel away from his face, he heard something other than the gun going off. He heard shoes scraping against the scuffed hardwood floor. Then something struck Walter's back. It didn't knock him out; he remained conscious, his eyes full of rage as he stared at Neil. But his grip loosened enough on the gun that Neil was able to take control of it and finally direct the barrel toward Walter.

"Stop," he warned him. "I will shoot you…"

He would do whatever was necessary to keep Elise safe and to be able to see her again.

Walter must not have believed him, though, because he reached again for the gun. Before Neil could pull the trigger, more noise erupted inside the cabin. Wood splintered as the door was kicked open, and the police officers rushed into the one-room cabin, their weapons drawn.

"Put it down, put it down!" they yelled at him.

"I'm Neil Colton," he identified himself.

He wasn't sure if the officer believed him or not, as the man took the gun from his hand while the other officer helped Walter up from the floor. Handcuffs snapped around Walter's wrists, though, while the other officer merely helped Neil to his feet, asking, "Are you okay?"

He nodded but peered around him to where Seth had slipped back to the floor. "He needs an ambulance, though." Walter had nearly killed his former son-in-law before Neil had even stepped inside the cabin. But he somehow felt responsible.

Had he gotten Seth too good a deal? Had justice not been served as Walter maintained? The older man kept shouting, "Let him die! Let him die!" His voice cracked with sobs, but he continued, "He shouldn't be alive when my sweet Leah is dead. None of you should."

"I didn't do it," Seth murmured from the floor.

But Neil still couldn't be certain. There had been so much evidence to indicate otherwise. Walter, obviously, had been convinced—so convinced that he'd tried to deliver his own form of justice.

To Seth and to Neil and Elise...

"What about the mayor?" Neil asked the officer. "Is she with you? Is she okay?"

The officer nodded. "Probably just pissed that we left her locked in the back of the car."

"Thank you," Neil said. They had protected her while he'd just put her in danger over and over again.

It was no wonder that she kept turning down his proposal. Not only didn't she trust that he loved her, she didn't trust that he could take care of her.

He understood. If not for Seth rallying enough to hit Walter, he might have gotten shot or worse. Killed…

He shuddered in reaction to the close call he'd just had. He'd had too damn many of them lately.

"Are you sure you're all right?" the officer asked.

No. He wasn't—because now that he'd realized why Elise kept turning down his proposal, he wasn't sure what he would ever be able to do to make her change her mind.

Elise had been home for hours, but she still couldn't stop shaking, couldn't stop reliving those moments she'd heard the gunshots and believed Neil was dead.

That she would never see him again…

But when she could have seen him again, she'd refused. Her fear, her emotions, had been too raw for her to trust herself. The minute he'd walked out of the cabin looking just a little mussed but overall healthy, she'd pleaded with another officer to drive her home.

Since she was the mayor, he'd been quick to agree—quick enough that Neil hadn't had time to stop her from leaving. But would he have tried?

She wondered now, since she'd been home for a while and he hadn't called, hadn't even texted. Was he mad at her for leaving?

Did he think she didn't care about him?

Because she cared—too damn much. She couldn't handle him putting himself in danger again. She just couldn't handle him.

Hunger, for which she liked to blame the baby, had finally taken her mind off what had happened, and she busied herself in the kitchen. After eating a bowl of chili she'd made and leaving the rest of the pot to simmer on low on a stove burner, she whipped together and rolled out some dough for Christmas cookies. It was not the first batch she'd made. While she considered before Thanksgiving too early to start decorating for Christmas, she never considered it too early to start baking for Christmas.

Her mom had taught her to cook and bake, but it wasn't something Elise had often done when she was married. She hadn't ever wanted to be a traditional wife who gave up or back-burnered her career to support her husband and take care of the children.

That was why she'd wanted to wait to start their family—until she'd established herself in Braxville. Until she was more than Neil Colton's wife and business partner.

She'd done that. She was the mayor.

And soon she would be a mother.

She wasn't sure she ever wanted to be a wife again, though—that she would ever be willing to risk her heart. Wadding up the leftover cookie dough, she popped it into her mouth just as the doorbell rang.

She'd left the crime scene earlier without giving a statement, so it could have been Jordana or Detective Carpenter following up with her. Leaving the stove and the oven on, she headed toward the door. The police interview would not take long; she hadn't seen anything. And she'd only heard that shot.

She flinched now as she relived that moment when fear that Neil was dead had slapped her like a physical blow. Her face might have still been in a grimace when she opened the door because the first question fired at her was, "Are you okay?"

Jordana wasn't the Colton who asked it, though. Neil stood outside her door. Then, uninvited, he stepped inside and closed the door behind himself. His hair was damp; maybe it was raining outside. Or maybe he'd recently showered...

The thought of which had an image popping into her mind, of him naked, water sluicing over his lean muscles.

"Elise?" He reached out for her, but she stepped back.

If he touched her, she wouldn't be able to resist him, not when she wanted him so damn much.

He flinched now. "I'm sorry," he said. "I won't."

"Won't what?" she asked. Make her want him? That wasn't possible.

"I won't push you," he said.

She snorted. "Of course not. You'd be worried about hurting the baby." The flash of jealousy she felt for her own child embarrassed and disgusted her. So she turned to head back toward her kitchen and the cookies she'd left in the oven.

He followed her but more slowly than she'd ever seen him move. As she took the cookie sheet from the oven, she studied his face. Dark circles rimmed those beautiful blue eyes of his, and his usually neatly clipped reddish beard was longer than usual.

"Are you okay?" she asked.

He shook his head.

And she gasped with concern. "I didn't think you were hurt." If she had, she wouldn't have left the scene.

"That's why you took off?" Neil asked. "It wasn't because…" He drew in a deep breath as if bracing himself for whatever he was going to say.

She held up a hand to stave off another proposal. "Now is not the time to bring up marriage."

"I wasn't going to," he said. "In fact, I'm taking back my proposal."

Skeptical, she narrowed her eyes and studied his handsome, exhausted face. "You are? Really?"

He nodded. "I realize what a fool I've been, Elise."

She sucked in a breath now, her heart and her pride stinging. "So wanting to marry me is foolish."

"You must think so, too, or you would have said yes," he murmured. "You wouldn't be getting so angry every time I propose. I figured that was why you had one of the police officers drive you away from the cabin. You were angry with me."

"I still am," she admitted. "You put your life in danger over and over again."

"I was a fool," he said, more easily now. "I'm lucky I didn't get killed or get you killed."

"What about Seth?" she asked. "Is Costner going to be okay?"

He nodded. "Yes. He's really beat up and still professing his innocence."

"Do you believe him?" she asked.

He shrugged. "I don't want to believe I convinced an innocent man to serve prison time."

"There was so much evidence," she reminded him.

"Too much," he said. "I lean more toward his guilt, but I suspect it was in the heat of the moment, not pre-meditated."

"So he served the correct sentence." She was glad of that; she would have hated to send an innocent man to prison, as well. Keeping the innocent free had been the reason she'd wanted to go into criminal law. Unfortunately, more of the guilty had wanted their representation than the innocent.

"I'm going to be more careful when I take on clients from now on," he said.

"And wives?" she quipped. "Since you've rescinded your proposal."

"You were never going to accept," he said. "I realized that, too, when I understood what a fool I've been. I realized that you're never going to trust me."

She sucked in another breath. "What happened in that cabin?" she asked. "How did you come to so many revelations? Did you get hit over the head? Near-death?"

Maybe he had been seriously hurt. She stepped closer to him and noticed the blood smeared on his hand. It might not have been his, but it looked fresh, like it was trickling down his arm as it had after the shooting in the garage. She gasped. "You're bleeding!"

He glanced down at his arm as if just noticing it. "That cut must have opened up again."

"How?" she asked.

"When I was wrestling with Shultz over the gun."

She closed her eyes as emotion overwhelmed her. She had come so close to losing him forever. But he wasn't hers. He hadn't been hers since the divorce.

"I'm sorry," he said. "I'm sorry I put myself in that position and worried you."

"What would I tell our child?" she wondered. "What would I say about his or her father if the baby is born after you're dead?"

His lips curved into a slight grin. "I imagine you could say a lot of things about what an idiot I've been."

"You're one of the smartest people I know," she said. Once she'd gotten to know him, she'd fallen even harder for his intelligence and wit than she had for his good looks.

"But I do stupid things," he said. "The stupidest thing I've ever done was divorce you."

A pang struck her heart. "Neil…"

He held up a hand now. "I'm not going to pressure you for anything anymore," he assured her. "I was a fool to pressure you to have kids right away."

"That's why you divorced me…" And since he was being so honest, she felt like she should be, too. "Because I wasn't enough for you."

"Oh, God, Elise, I was afraid that's what you were thinking," he said. "When I was having all these revelations, I realized you must think the only reason I want to marry you again is because of the baby."

"It is," she said. And she was certain. Too certain for him to convince her otherwise, not that she expected him to try.

He closed his eyes now, as if reeling from the same emotions rushing over her. "It's not. I wanted to marry you again the minute I divorced you. Hell, I never really wanted to divorce you."

"You just wanted me to have a baby before I was ready," she said. "And if you loved me, really loved me, you wouldn't have pressured me."

"I did really love you," he insisted. "But I was also impatient and selfish and wanted what I wanted when I wanted it."

"Did? Was? You've changed?" she challenged him.

His lips curved into that grin. "I will," he promised. "That's why I rescinded my proposal—to prove it. I won't pressure you anymore."

She touched her stomach, which was full of the chili and the cookies. "Because you're getting what you want, the baby you want."

"I want a family," Neil said. "That's what I wanted then and what I want now. I wanted a real family—with love and affection between the parents and time and attention given freely to the children."

A pang struck her heart. "Neil…"

She'd always envied his childhood, how he'd had the big, boisterous family. But she hadn't been part of that family for very long before realizing that his parents really weren't happy together, and their tense relationship must have affected all the kids. Neil more than she'd realized.

"I'm sorry," she said.

He shook his head. "You had it far worse than I did," he said. "Being just you and your mom."

But now she wondered. Sure, her mother had had to work hard, menial jobs to support them, but Elise had never had any doubt that she was loved. And since it had been just the two of them, there had been nothing but love.

"I hadn't wanted to wind up like your parents, either," she admitted. "That's why I didn't fight the divorce. I didn't want there to be that cold resentment between us."

He shivered and nodded. "Me, neither. That was why I filed, but I'd hoped you'd change your mind. And I'm sorry for that—for trying to manipulate you to get what I wanted."

"I wanted a family, too," she said. "I just wanted to wait to find myself and to forge my career. I didn't want to have to make the sacrifices my mother made."

"I know," he said. "And I wish I'd been patient."

She chuckled. "That's just not you."

"It will be," he promised. "I won't pressure you ever again."

She narrowed her eyes and studied his handsome face again. "Is this a manipulation to get what you want? To get me to accept your proposal?"

He sighed. "I deserve that…after the things I've done. But no, I rescinded my proposal and I won't ask again."

"Then what do you want, Neil?"

He shook his head. "It doesn't matter what I want. I want to know what you want. Do you want me to leave you alone?"

That was the last thing she wanted. But she wasn't ready yet to admit it. She wasn't sure if she believed in his turnaround, and she worried that she might never completely trust him.

"You're bleeding on my floor. I want you to go the doctor and have your arm stitched back up," she said.

He nodded and turned as if heading toward the door. That easily? Without an argument?

"Neil?"

He turned back, his eyes bright with hope. "Is there something else you want, Elise?"

Him. But not now, not when he was hurt and exhausted and she wasn't sure this was real or just brought on by his close call.

"Time," she said. "I want time to think…" Time to trust.

He nodded. "Let me know when you want to see me again."

"What about our standing dinner?" she asked.

"You still want to do that?"

Every month she looked forward to meeting up, to talking and arguing and entertaining each other over a meal. And last month they'd made a baby.

"Yes. I'm not angry with you," she assured him.

"You just don't trust me," he stated as a fact.

Maybe he knew her better than she'd realized. Of course, that had been one of his revelations—that she didn't trust him.

"Not yet," she admitted, then warned him, "and maybe not ever."

He flinched. "I deserve that. I made a lot of mistakes, but if you'll give me a chance, date me, I'll prove to you that I can be patient, that I can put your needs first."

He'd always done that in the bedroom. Maybe it was possible that he could do it in other aspects of their lives.

She drew in a shaky breath and nodded. "It's a date, then."

"Friday night?"

She nodded and waited for him to close the distance between them, to kiss her. But he turned away again and headed toward the door.

And a curious mixture of disappointment and hope coursed through her. Could it be different this time? Could they actually make it work if they tried again?

She was afraid to hope that it was—afraid of being devastated again like she'd been when he'd divorced her. But she owed it to herself and to their unborn baby to give him a chance to prove it to her. To prove that he understood and loved her...

"Your son is in the ER again," a young nurse informed Lilly, making her heart flip with fear.

She hurried from the empty training room down to the bustling emergency room. Where was he? What had happened now? She'd thought it was all over—that the person trying to kill him and Elise had been caught. When she found which ER unit he'd been assigned, she jerked open the curtain to see him, to see how badly he was hurt.

Again.

A resident leaned over Neil's arm, stitching up a small wound. "Your son is giving me a lot of practice," the young woman said with a chuckle.

Lilly couldn't laugh with her, not over this. "Too much practice."

"It's over, Mom," Neil assured her. "The guy that was after us is in jail now."

"I know," she said. "Jordana told me."

He winced, and she doubted it was because of the needle piercing his skin. This resident would have made certain he was numb before she started stitching. "I'm sorry," he said. "I should have called you and Dad."

It was her turn to wince now. She hadn't told Fitz yet. Maybe Jordana had called him, too, though.

She glanced around the waiting room. "Is Elise here?"

He shook his head. "She wasn't hurt."

"That's good," she said. "But I thought that maybe you two were back together. I was hoping that she'd come to Christmas dinner with you."

"I was hoping that, too," he said. "But we're not back together."

Lilly stepped closer and squeezed his free hand. "I'm sorry. I know how much you love her." And how much he was going to need her and not just for the holidays, but for support to deal with everything that was about to be revealed.

Too many secrets had been kept for too damn long...

"I do love her," Neil said. "But she doesn't trust my love anymore. And I'm not going to convince her by pressuring her. I'm going to show her that I love her by giving her what she needs. Patience."

The resident emitted a wistful sigh. And Lilly smiled in approval. "Good. She loves you, too. She'll come around." Or maybe all those damn secrets would push her farther away from Neil and the Coltons.

As the mayor, Elise couldn't subject herself to the scandal that was becoming their lives.

Neil squeezed Lilly's hand as if he suspected she had doubts. "She will," he said, but he sounded as if he was trying to convince himself as much as he was her.

She pondered telling Neil the truth now, so that he would have a chance to do the right thing for Elise and for her career. But one of the secrets, the worst one, wasn't hers to tell.

Chapter 27

Maybe it was the candlelight. Maybe it was the pregnancy, but Elise was glowing. Just radiant.

She raised her hand to her face and touched her mouth. "Do I have something in my teeth?" she asked. "Or did I dribble on my chin?"

Too overwhelmed with her beauty to speak, he just shook his head.

"What is it?" she asked. "You're staring."

"You're beautiful," he murmured in awe.

Her green eyes narrowed, and she stared at him. "Are you trying to manipulate me again?"

A pang struck his heart—of regret and despair. "You're never going to trust me," he said. It didn't matter how slow he went, how little pressure he exerted. "You're never going to accept my proposal."

"You rescinded it," she reminded him. With—*was that*—a trace of disappointment?

If she was disappointed, maybe she had been more tempted to accept than he'd realized. Or he was just grasping at straws.

But Elise was the one grasping the straw in a tall glass. Closing her eyes, she took a long draw and moaned in delight.

And his body tightened with desire. She was so damn beautiful, so sensual…even more so now that she was glowing. It wasn't fair. How could he be patient when it was killing him not to touch her, to taste her?

She swiped her tongue across her bottom lip. "You sure you don't want to try this shake?" she asked. "Eggnog. It's so good."

He wanted to taste it but not through the straw. He wanted to taste it on her lips, on her tongue…in her mouth. "Elise…" He cleared the desire from his throat. "I'm not an eggnog fan."

"You don't know what you're missing."

But he knew all too well. He was missing her. He'd been missing her since she'd moved out of their house, and not just since the other night but since he'd done the stupidest thing he'd ever done: filed for divorce.

But he couldn't tell her that—it would be manipulative. So he pushed aside how much he wanted her, how much he ached to be with her again. And he asked about her running the city and even about Jeremy and he told her about the practice, about his new client—the single mom going after her kids' father for back child support.

"It's not criminal," she remarked.

"No, it is," he insisted. "It's criminal that he's not helping her raise their kids—not physically and not financially." But Neil was going to make certain that he helped—whether the man wanted to or not. "I hope that's not why you were nervous about having kids with me, because you thought I might take off like your dad did."

She flinched and pushed away her shake, as if she suddenly felt queasy.

He did, his stomach clenching with dread that she'd had such doubts about him.

"I just wanted to wait until I was sure of *me*," she said.

"You can be sure of me, too," he said. "Sure that I love you for you. Always have. Always will. From the first moment I saw you."

She giggled. "Staring at you…you caught me staring…"

"Like you just caught me," he said. "You're so beautiful. Believe that. Believe how amazing you are. How smart, how sexy, how…" Desire choked him, making his voice trail off.

Elise's beautiful eyes glistened with tears, and she jumped up from her chair and rushed toward the exit.

Neil groaned. He'd done it again. While he was just being honest about how he felt about her, she must have considered it another manipulation to push her into what he wanted. So he resisted his impulse to chase her out of the restaurant. They'd met there, each driving their recently repaired vehicles, so she could drive herself home.

Once he'd paid the bill and left the restaurant, he resisted the urge to drive to her condo to apologize to her. She would probably construe that as pushing her again.

He needed to give Elise space, but staying away from her was so damn hard.

Especially now when he realized what a fool he'd been and how much he wanted—*needed*—to be with her—forever. While he wouldn't let himself go to her house, he didn't want to go home, either—to that empty house they'd been supposed to share.

But where else could he go? To his parents'? To his siblings'? It wasn't as if any of them was going to give him the sympathy or encouragement he wanted. Most either thought he was a fool for divorcing Elise, or, in his father's case, a fool for marrying her in the first place.

The family Christmas party was soon, so he would see them all then. But he would be attending alone…

He hadn't even had the chance to ask Elise to join him for the celebration. Not that she probably would have accepted anyway. And he couldn't blame her—after all the mistakes he'd made.

It didn't matter how long he drove around town or whom he went to see, he wasn't going to be thinking of anyone but Elise, of anything but how badly he'd screwed up. So he might as well go home.

Not that it had felt like a home since she'd moved out. He should have sold it then. But he'd really believed they'd get back together, that she would move back in.

Maybe it was time to accept reality. She was never going to trust him. She couldn't even trust that he was telling the truth when he complimented her.

The garage door opened as the SUV neared it, and he pulled inside the recently cleaned space. All the glass was gone now, his vehicle repaired. So everything was back to the way that it had been before Walter Shultz had come after them—everything but him.

He was different. He only wished Elise could see that.

The minute he stepped inside the house, he felt something was different about it. It didn't feel empty…like he'd dreaded it would, like it had for the past few years.

But was that a good thing or a bad thing?

Had someone gotten inside while he'd been gone?

The alarm wasn't going off, but a lot of people knew his security code. One of them could have gotten in without setting off the alarm.

His pulse quickened with excitement. Not fear.

Walter Shultz was in jail and had been denied bail. He couldn't get out. Not that Neil couldn't have another enemy…

As he walked through the mudroom to the kitchen, he noticed a strange multicolored glow. Then he heard the music playing softly, charmingly…

Christmas music.

Christmas lights.

As he walked past the island in the kitchen, he noticed the tray of cookies sitting on it. And a smile curved his lips and his pulse pounded now with excitement, with anticipation.

When he stepped into the great room, Elise raised her hands with an ornament dangling from one finger. "Don't shoot," she said. "I'm not here to hurt you."

"I'm the one who keeps hurting you," he said, his heart heavy with regret for all the mistakes he'd made. "I'm sorry I sent you running out of the restaurant."

She shook her head. "I was just overwhelmed..."

"And I didn't mean to do that," he said. "I didn't mean to pressure you."

"I know..."

But did she? Did she know how much he loved her?

Afraid to give in to hope, he had to ask, "Why are you here?"

She pointed toward the tree. "We never finished decorating."

He stepped closer and repeated, "Why are you here, Elise?"

Elise drew in a deep breath to settle the nerves fluttering around in her stomach. Then she realized she wasn't nervous. Not at all...

Because she trusted Neil and, more important, she trusted his love.

Maybe the fluttering in her stomach was the baby, then. Maybe worrying about losing him or her these past few weeks had made her more sensitive to his or her movements.

Or maybe she'd eaten too much at dinner and too many Christmas cookies since then.

"Elise?" Neil prodded her. "Why are you here?"

She smiled at him, at the tension on his handsome face. He looked nervous.

She was not, as she dropped to her knees in front

of him. "You rescinded your proposal, so I'm offering mine."

His brow furrowed with confusion. "What?"

"Will you marry me, Neil Colton?"

"You're proposing to me?" he asked, his voice gruff.

She nodded. "You said you wouldn't propose to me again."

"Not until you were ready," he said.

"I'm ready," she said.

He shook his head. "This is too soon. I promised I wasn't going to pressure you. I was going to give you time."

"You did," she said.

He snorted. "Barely a week."

"You gave me three years," she said. "Three years to find out who I am without you."

His lips curved into a slight smile. "The mayor. You're pretty damn powerful."

She nodded. "Yes, I am. I'm not going to lose myself this time."

"You didn't lose yourself last time, Elise," he said.

"No, I didn't," she said. "And I survived when we were apart."

His brow furrowed again. "So why are you proposing, then? Is this because you don't want to be a single parent?"

Shock gripped her; she was stunned that he had the same doubts about her love that she'd had about his. Until tonight, when she'd seen how he'd stared at her.

And she'd remembered that he'd always looked at her that way—with love.

"Whether we're married or not, I would never be a single parent when you're the father of this baby," she said. "I know that you would never abandon a child the way my father abandoned me. You are too good a man to ever do that. You're such a good man, Neil Colton, that you put your life on the line for me and for our baby and even for Seth Costner when you have no idea if he's guilty or innocent. I love you."

His breath shuddered out in a ragged sigh of relief. And he dropped to his knees in front of her. "And I love you, Elise. I always have and I always will, and I hope you believe that."

"I do…"

"Will you say that again as soon as we can get down to City Hall and make this official?"

"Are you accepting my proposal?" she asked.

"Hell yes," he said, and he lowered his mouth to hers.

She kissed him back with all the passion and love she felt for him. He groaned and murmured her name, and his hands shook a little as he fumbled to undress her and him…until they were naked but for the glow of the multicolored lights on their skin.

Neil pushed her gently back onto the rug and he showed her how much he loved her by giving her more pleasure than she'd thought it was possible to experience. And she wondered how she had ever doubted his feelings even during and after the divorce. Because she could feel his love for her as fiercely as she felt hers for him.

"I love you," she cried out as another orgasm shuddered through her body. Then he was inside her, filling her as completely as he always had. They moved together, in sync, finding the rhythm that led to another release for her and one for him that had him shouting her name and his love for her.

Then he held her closely as if he never intended to let her go. But it didn't matter; she had no intention of going anywhere. She was right where she wanted to be—in his arms.

Seated at the head of the dining room table, Fitz Colton usually felt like a king surveying his empire. That was what his family felt like to him—something he'd built, like he'd built so many other things. Since last Christmas his empire had grown, and many more people sat around the long table. Significant others of his kids. His brother…

But this Christmas, he didn't feel like a king sitting on his throne; he felt more as if he was seated in the witness chair during a trial—his.

Maybe that was because there were two lawyers at his table now. His son Neil but also Neil's once-again wife, Elise. Even though she was now the mayor, or maybe because of it, Elise scrutinized him with an unsettling intensity. She knew something was up.

But how could she not, with everything that had happened in Braxville over the past several months?

Some of it had been terrible, like that maniac trying to kill her and Neil. Some had been wonderful, like the fact that she was pregnant with his first grandchild. He smiled at her, and her eyes widened for a moment with surprise before she smiled back.

A tinkling of glass drew his attention to the other side of the table across from Elise and Neil. Bridgette lightly struck her wine goblet with a fork. "I have an announcement to make," she said. Then she reached for Luke Walker's hand.

Fitz still wasn't entirely sure how his daughter had fallen for the owner of the local hardware store, but she had rented an apartment from him. And like his father, who'd worked for Fitz, Luke was a damn nice guy. Good looking, too, with his light brown hair and green eyes.

"We have an announcement to make." Bridgette held up their joined hands and a diamond sparkled on hers. "We're engaged!"

Cheers and shouts rang out around the table as they had moments earlier, when Neil and Elise had announced their happy news.

This news didn't make him as happy as the baby news had. But then he hadn't quite forgiven Bridgette for her investigation shutting down his business. "So who's moving?" Fitz asked the couple.

Bridgette smiled. "Me. I'll be working out of the field office in Wichita and commuting from Braxville."

"We'll be building a house soon," Luke added.

"I would have offered to build it for you," Fitz said, "like I did Neil and Elise's—if you hadn't opened that investigation and shut down my company."

"Stop it!" Lilly yelled as she jumped up from her chair at the other end of the long table. "Stop it!"

Shame gripped him, and he knew she was right. It was time.

"Stop blaming Bridgette or Elise or the previous

mayor or even Dex for what you did…" she said, and tears began to stream down her face. "Tell them the truth."

"I—I thought we were going to wait until after the holidays," he reminded her of the promise he'd extracted from her when he'd finally told her the truth.

She shook her head and a tendril of deep red hair slipped free of the knot she'd bound it in and trailed down her face like the tears. "I didn't agree to that. Now is the time…when we're all together."

While he stared at his wife of so many years, the rest of the family were all staring at him as if they already knew. Maybe they did or at least suspected.

"What is it, Dad?" Neil asked.

Fitz expelled a shaky sigh and cleared his throat. "I might know why my former employees have gotten sick," he admitted.

Bridgette gasped, and Luke slid his arm around her, holding her close. One of those employees who'd gotten sick was Luke's father.

"Twenty-five years ago the company was struggling," he said. He gestured around the table. "We were struggling. With all you kids and all the expenses, I couldn't afford to lose the business, so I cut some corners."

"What kind of corners?" Bridgette asked.

"I bought some construction materials from overseas," he replied. "Materials that weren't subjected to the same guidelines and inspections as the materials here…"

Bridgette understood more than the rest of them, because she clasped a hand over her mouth, as if to hold back another gasp or a cry.

"I wouldn't have used them if I'd thought they would make people sick," he said. He hadn't wanted anyone to get hurt, but he could see that he had hurt not just his employees but his family, as well.

Especially his family.

He closed his eyes as shame overwhelmed him. A strong hand grabbed his shoulder, squeezing. He opened his eyes, expecting to find Shep offering him comfort. If only Shep had helped him with the business instead of joining the Navy...

But it wasn't Shep standing over him. It was Neil.

"You need to make a full confession to the authorities," Neil said. "I'll go with you. I'll represent you."

Fitz sucked in a breath of shock. "I—I'm not ready."

It was bad enough that his family knew. If everyone else learned the truth...

"It's going to come out," Elise said.

Now he didn't give a damn that she carried his grandchild; he glared at her. "I thought I could trust you—now that you're a Colton again."

"I'm still Mayor Willis," she reminded him. "And I have a duty to protect this town. Do I need to shut down the mall, Fitz?"

He groaned and turned toward Bridgette.

"What was it, Dad?" she asked. "What kind of materials did you bring in?"

"Treated lumber."

She gasped. "Arsenic...that's what's getting everybody." She turned toward her fiancé. "I'm sorry..."

"It's not your fault," Fitz said. "It's not any of your faults. I brought in Dex and I thought he would help, but he was all talk and empty promises. And I had to figure out how to keep those promises or lose the business." Instead two people had lost their lives, and so many more had gotten sick. He knew now that what he'd done was wrong. "I can't undo it," he said. "I can't go back and change the past. What will it matter if we wait another week?"

"I'm shutting down the mall," Elise murmured.

"We already checked it once," Bridgette said. "The levels weren't too high. Most of the wood would have been covered up. We'll see what we need to do."

His family was going to work together to make right what he'd ruined. Fitz saw that now as his children all began to talk at once, to each other and to the new loves in their lives. Only Lilly didn't speak to him; she spoke to his brother instead. She couldn't even look at him anymore.

Fitz accepted then what he had known for a while. His life as he knew it was over. Nothing would ever be the same.

* * * * *

Don't miss the exciting conclusion of
The Coltons of Kansas
with Cindy Dees's

Colton in the Line of Fire

Available from Harlequin Romantic Suspense!

#2115 COLTON 911: ULTIMATE SHOWDOWN
Colton 911: Grand Rapids • by Addison Fox
When Grand Rapid's most beloved CSI investigator, Sadie Colton, is in danger, the only one who can protect her is Lieutenant Tripp McKellar. She's always had a soft spot for Tripp but she treads carefully, given his tragic past—and hers. Can she hide her feelings as the threat against her comes bearing down on them both?

#2116 COLTON IN THE LINE OF FIRE
The Coltons of Kansas • by Cindy Dees
While investigating a cold case, lab technician Yvette Colton finally tells overbearing detective Reese Carpenter to back off her work. But Reese is beginning to realize his frustration may have been hiding softer feelings toward Yvette. As the cold case suddenly turns hot, he'll have to help manage an invisible threat and protect Yvette at all costs...

#2117 OPERATION MOUNTAIN RECOVERY
Cutter's Code • by Justine Davis
A random stop leads Brady Crenshaw, a tough, experienced deputy, to a shocking accident. As he fights to bring Ashley Jordan back from the brink of death, he discovers an even greater danger than an icy cliff. It's unclear whom exactly she needs protecting from—and how deeply Brady might be involved.

#2118 ESCAPE WITH THE NAVY SEAL
The Riley Code • by Regan Black
Navy SEAL Mark Riley was almost excited to finally face the man targeting his father—until an innocent civilian was taken along with him. He didn't expect to brave close confines with Charlotte Hanover—or the bond they forged together. Now he and Charlotte must escape a prison island with only their wits and his military experience to help them!

HRSCNM1120

"Do you remember that summer we turned my mom's minivan into a fort?" Mark asked.

"We? That was all you and Luke." Charlotte closed her eyes, recalling those sweet days.

"You were there," Mark said. "Guilt by association."

"Maybe so." She opened her eyes. "This place could do with some pilfered couch cushions and a hanging sheet or two."

Mark chuckled. "And gummy bears."

"Yes." She rolled her wrists, trying to get some relief from the handcuffs. "What made you think of Fort Van... whatever it was?"

"Fort Van Dodge," he supplied. "You slept in there. I remember your eyelashes."

She sat up and blinked said lashes, wishing for better light to read his expression. "What are you talking about?"

He rested his head against the panel. "Your eyelashes turned into little gold fans on your cheeks when you slept. Still happens, I bet."

Weary and uncertain, she drew his words straight into her heart. She should probably find something witty to say or a memory to share, but her adrenaline spikes were giving way to pure exhaustion. Better to stay quiet than say something that made him feel obligated to take on more of her stress.

"Sleep if you can," Mark said, as if he'd read her mind. "I won't let anything happen."

He clearly wanted to spare her, and she appreciated his efforts, but she had a feeling it would take both of them working together to escape this mess.

Don't miss
Escape with the Navy SEAL *by Regan Black,
available December 2020 wherever
Harlequin Romantic Suspense
books and ebooks are sold.*

Harlequin.com

Get 4 FREE REWARDS!

We'll send you 2 FREE Books plus 2 FREE Mystery Gifts.

Harlequin Romantic Suspense books are heart-racing page-turners with unexpected plot twists and irresistible chemistry that will keep you guessing to the very end.

FREE Value Over $20

Love Harlequin romance?

DISCOVER.

Be the first to find out about promotions, news and exclusive content!

Facebook.com/HarlequinBooks

Twitter.com/HarlequinBooks

Instagram.com/HarlequinBooks

Pinterest.com/HarlequinBooks

ReaderService.com

EXPLORE.

Sign up for the Harlequin e-newsletter and download a free book from any series at **TryHarlequin.com**

CONNECT.

Join our Harlequin community to share your thoughts and connect with other romance readers!
Facebook.com/groups/HarlequinConnection